LUCY CROWE

LUCY CROWE

ADIR E GOLAN

Hagdyl Benem

This is a work of fiction. All of the characters, organizations and events portrayed in this novel are either products of the author's imagination or used fictitiously.

LUCY CROWE

A Hagdyl Benem Book.

First Edition: 21 October 2025
ISBNs: 979-8-9928584-2-6 (paperback), 979-8-9928584-0-2 (ebook)

To Mom and Dad
who gave me the pages
that would become my first book

- The Last Straw -

Lucy. Lucy. LUCY! Why won't you talk to us Lucy? We miss you... Don't you miss us!? Lucy. Lucy. LUCY.

Her breaths quickened. She didn't want this—couldn't deal with this. Not now, in front of everyone.

Something smashed into the window. Everyone turned to see a dead crow, twitching, leaving a crack in the glass along with a smudge of blood. They all returned to their task at hand, scribbling away.

Prelims.

Lucy Crowe gawked at the spot where the bird hit just a few seconds more. Someone she knew loved crows. Someone that was bothering her far too often lately; her voice far too loud.

Sweat beaded on Lucy's forehead as she pressed pen to paper so hard that a blotch of ink bled onto the tearing page. The gooey smudge began to rearrange itself, the erratic scribbles of her name slinking back to the point of origin.

Oozing, a tendril wound out, then another. Tiny ink spiders crawled out of the stain, rapidly, running up Lucy's arm.

She did her best to ignore what she felt creeping on her skin. She *knew* it wasn't real. Neither were the whispers that bounced off the walls, getting louder and louder, chanting Lucy's name until it became a cacophony.

But it didn't stop. It just got stronger. More spiders tickling her flesh. More whispers. Calling her name again and again and again—

"Shut up!" Lucy screamed, swore, standing, "SHUT UP!"

The voices listened. Utter silence followed.

Too silent.

Not even the scratching of pen on paper could be heard. This was bad. Tentative, Lucy opened her eyes, very slowly, hands almost numb, dropping limply at her side.

Yes, everyone was staring at her.

Lucy lay on her bed, face buried in her pillow. A knock came at the door. She didn't bother responding and neither did her mother, Mary, bother waiting for an answer.

"Lucy?" she asked.

"Not now, Mum," her voice came muffled.

"The principal called, said you swore at everyone in the middle of your prelim, then ran out." Mary sounded more concerned than indignant.

Lucy felt her sitting on the bed. Even though she didn't want anyone near her right now, it was nice not being alone.

"They're at it again, aren't they?"

Reluctantly, Lucy finally rolled over, looking to her mother with a heavy sigh.

Dr Gray's office was a place Lucy never wanted to visit again. She thought she'd never have to. She realised how foolish that was as she sat in the plain space, medical books littering the shelf behind him. Beyond stereotypical. So was his receding hairline, hooked nose, spectacles and deep laugh lines. He looked a little like a villain from a movie she'd seen a while back, he was somewhat charismatic.

On the chair beside Lucy, Mary seemed devastated yet determined as Dr Gray rambled on. He wasn't worried, though. There were options for treatment.

Lucy wasn't really paying attention. She'd heard it all before over the last ten years. Besides, she was distracted. Just behind the doctor, she could see herself standing.

Well, it wasn't really her, to be precise. That was Lucifera. She looked the exact same, had the same British accent. Now she even donned the same clothes, though she didn't always. Lucifera also wore a mischievous glare, which was never a good sign.

"We were always there for you, Lucy," she sneered. "The best of friends growing up."

Absent-minded, Lucy snatched some medication that Dr Gray handed her. She tried to ignore her doppelgänger, who shook her head adamantly.

"Don't do it," she warned.

Her mother gave her a bottle of water, urging. Lucy hesitated, swallowing a pang of guilt. How could she turn her back on them? They were her best friends, there for her in the hardest of times.

Lucifera watched her with a stark expression. Unwavering. Heart of stone.

"I just want to be normal," Lucy said finally. She placed the pink pill on her tongue. It started becoming bitter.

"Normal?" Lucifera bent to reach behind Dr Gray's chair from where she lifted a battle axe. "Well, if you ask me, normal's no fun at all."

Lucy swallowed a sip of water.

Lucifera shrugged, then swung the axe at the doctor's neck.

Lucy shut her eyes at the sound of the weapon's impact. Felt specks of something warm on her face. But it wasn't real. It wasn't real...

- Chapter One -
"Old News"

Eyes sealed tight, breathing deep, Lucinda "Lucy" Crowe sat in the back seat of a taxi. At thirty, she was a well-rounded career woman, with a blonde bob cut and deep green eyes. She wore a suit today.

Driven. Beautiful. *Normal*.

"Yoohoo! Lady..." She heard the taxi driver, "I know your guests aren't going anywhere, but I don't have all day."

Lucy opened her eyes and nodded slowly at the chubby, balding man in the driver's seat. She clutched her door's handle, shook her head. Nope. She was too nervous. It all rushed back.

Sighing, looking to the sides like he shouldn't be doing it, the taxi driver opened his cubbyhole, passing Lucy a hip flask. The kind man shook it a little, giving a half smile.

It couldn't hurt, right? Lucy accepted the offer, took a sip. She hated bourbon. She gulped a mouthful. Cringed.

Okay, now she was ready to face them. As she stepped out the driver came to hoot but stopped himself at the last second, paying respect to the place they were in. "Psst!"

He held out the meagre bouquet Lucy had forgotten in the back seat. Two of the flowers sagged away from the rest.

Snatching them up with a grateful nod, she walked under the arched entrance of Brompton Cemetery.

She made her way through alleys of graves. It was so quiet here. So peaceful, like nature had given a pocket of otherworldly serenity to those who'd passed on. Lucy, however, was not at peace. Not even close. This was the hardest thing she'd done in years.

Coming to a stop in front of a tombstone, she studied it for a few long moments. It was adorned with symbols in each of the corners: a Celtic knot, a Star of David, a cross and a triskelion. An unexpected pang of emotion hit her. She'd come in previous years, inconsistently, whenever she really needed a reminder, but today was going to be her last time reopening these scarred wounds.

Lu, Luce, Lucy, Lucinda. 1995-2012.

Did a part of her miss them? Maybe some of them. And only sometimes. An old habit. What the hell kind of doctor recommends burying parts of you for "closure?" Perhaps Dr Gray was the real weirdo. It didn't matter though. His advice always worked. She'd managed to live a normal life. No thanks to those four names etched on that stone. No, life was good *in spite* of them.

An older man sauntered past, footsteps light. He stopped at Lucy's side, gaze shifting to the engraved stone. Slowly, empathetically, he shook his head. Lucy watched him, both of them silent at first.

"That should never happen," he said. "But they live on...in *here*." He smiled warmly at Lucy, touching his heart.

Did he think those were her kids? Who puts four names on a single tombstone?

"Oh, God—no..." Lucy interjected. "Couldn't wait to get rid of them. I'm just here for 'closure.'" She motioned air quotes, then tossed the sad bouquet on the grave and waded away, leaving the older man quite flabbergasted.

Maybe she should have explained more. Never mind, she'd never see him again. At that moment she decided she'd never visit the place again either. Dad wasn't buried there, so why should she ever stop by?

This was the last cycle of therapy in her opinion. Thirteen years of yearly visits was more than enough.

Once arriving at their destination just outside an apartment building, Lucy checked the meter and paid the driver. He tipped his hat because she gave him a little extra.

A creepy-ass grin stretched on his face, showing far too many teeth. Under the peak of his flat cap, his eyes were pitch black. Lucy blinked—and he was just the same old *normal* taxi driver.

She lived alone in a small place. Neat. Clean. Very regular. No pets, just a plant.

"Hello, Léon!" Smiling at the Chinese evergreen, she snatched a spray bottle and gave Léon a little misting.

A handsome vision board took up half the wall of her bedroom. It was titled *13 Years Free*. Lucy didn't glance at it now; she went straight into the en-suite bathroom and popped open her medicine cabinet.

Plucking two familiar companions from there, clozapine and St John's wort, she swallowed them with some water from the tap. The kind of thing that would always annoy her mother when she did it as a teen.

Lucy loved living alone, being in control of her own apartment. Lately, though, it started feeling lonely if she were being honest. But obviously today was one of those days. Funny how things could become sentimental even when they hurt you, leaving a part of you to miss them.

Stupid.

In Lucy's fridge, the top shelf had sealed Pyrex dishes with precooked meals. Same for the second shelf. On the door, jars packed with a week's supply of overnight oats. She cracked one open for breakfast.

Walking into the office building of Bender & Co. Accounting, Lucy smiled brightly at the clerk even though she didn't feel so bright.

"Morning, Jill!"

Jill was a friend. Not too close though. She had no idea of Lucy's condition, because she preferred not sharing too much. It added nothing, and usually didn't end well, with people either feeling sorry for her, which was awful, or they stayed away. Lucy would much rather avoid the whole scandal.

When the elevator doors closed, she glimpsed a narrow crack slither along the wall behind Jill, where the company's sign was plastered. It didn't excite Lucy; these little snippets came and went depending on how stressed she was. Mostly, they weren't even that noticeable. Just vestiges of her mind's bad old habits.

Lucy crunched numbers at her desk...

She took her pills in the bathroom... Ate breakfast in her kitchen... Greeted Jill at the company's foyer, where the crack had grown larger and wider.

Lucy crunched numbers at her desk.

Lucy taking pills. Eating breakfast. "Good morning" at work—larger crack.

Crunching numbers at her desk.

Pills—breakfast—"good morning"—spreading crack—numbers—

Pills. Crack. Breakfast. Crack. Numbers. CRACK.

Breaking an egg into a pan, Lucy moved lightly to the beat of instrumental Celtic music playing from a wireless speaker. A beep interrupted the tune, and she checked her mobile: a reminder for an appointment with Dr Gray.

"Oh, bloody hell!"

She ran to her bedroom, egg still sizzling in the frying pan. Hopping back into the kitchen, Lucy was busy putting on her second shoe, her jacket hanging off one arm. Swiping up her phone, she left the house.

Seconds later she rushed back in, turned off the stove, taking a banana instead.

St Bones Clinic was a place Lucy had become quite familiar with over the years. Her perception of it had changed from when she was seventeen. The clinic provided some form of solace now. She came here less and less. After her previous visit, they'd taken the usual blood work to make sure everything was in check.

Dr Gray was sixty now, hair matching his name. He still reminded Lucy of that actor a little...what was his name?

"You're looking great, Lucy," Dr Gray held open his office door for her. "Haven't seen you in a few months, which is good. What have you been up to?"

"You know. Work, the usual stuff," she took a seat.

"Anything exciting?"

"Thank God no."

Sitting behind his desk, Dr Gray lifted the glasses hanging around his neck, fixed them on his nose, and began perusing her folder. "How are the hallucinations?"

"Hardly even see them anymore."

Dr Gray nodded.

Lucy had the day off, maybe she'd go grocery shopping. Jill offered to take her ice-skating after she finished her shift. She'd text her after the meeting saying that she would join. That would be nice. She felt lighter since she'd made the decision to leave those annual cemetery visits behind.

"And the others? Making any appearances?"

Lucy shook her head.

"So, the St John's wort is working fine for you so far. That's good..." he trailed off, reading some more info.

St John's wort was a more natural alternative to a medication she used to take. It took some time to wean off slowly and the results weren't a sure thing when starting out. Now it was another positive step forward in her journey.

Still eyeing the file, Dr Gray scratched his chin. Lucy noticed it immediately. She was sort of afraid to ask.

"The test results, Dr Gray?"

Damn it, there was a pause. Short, yet felt like forever. She was starting to become conscious of her own heartbeat. She knew the kind of news she was going to get but was still on the edge of her seat, wondering just how severe this was.

"We've spoken about the risks of using clozapine, in the past," he said, "it's just that nothing else helped your episodes and—"

"Get to the point Doc," Lucy urged.

He took a beat to look at her. Dr Gray didn't seem to want to be the harbinger of this. Must have hated his job at that very moment.

"You have agranulocytosis," he said finally.

"What is that?"

"Your blood doesn't have enough infection-fighting cells."

"This is 'cause of the medication?"

Dr Gray didn't respond. He wasn't finished.

"What else?" she braced herself. It made no difference whatsoever.

"Cirrhosis of the liver."

Lucy gathered her thoughts—well, actually, there were none. Just white noise upstairs that dragged on for a bit like a needle reaching the end of a spinning record.

"All right, what do we need to do?" she asked, not digesting this. She needed a plan of action. Then she'd be able to wrap her head around it all. Just like her vision board back home, just like her multi-year process of healing, of following her dreams. One step at a time.

"At this point," said Dr Gray, "I'm afraid there's not much..."

"There has to be something we can do," Lucy said. She wasn't one to give up. Not after all she'd been through. No, her book still had several unwritten chapters outlined. She wanted to say more, her mouth was open. She just didn't know what words to use.

"I'm afraid..." he sighed, biting his jaw like he was pulling off a plaster, "I'm afraid you have no more than a year, Lucy."

She felt like she was hit by a double-decker bus.

"But I feel fine..."

"Great as that may be, it's no indication of what is happening inside your body."

Lucy wasn't even looking at him anymore. Her vision swirled a little. The room tilted for a moment, cracks spreading along the walls. She sluggishly blinked it away. She just heard ringing at this point. A high-pitched buzz that swelled, overwhelming.

She got up and left Dr Gray's office.

Dusk had come before she knew it. Time lost all meaning since she got the news. Numb, Lucy sat at the bus stop with that same vacant stare she had at Gray's practice.

A young guy with a tilted cap waddled past, eyeing her handbag on the bench. Lucy barely even noticed the bloke.

The youngster snatched her bag and dashed, not evoking any reaction.

A little further down the street, another pedestrian tackled the thief, gave him a good beating. Went a little too far, in fact. People just glanced and continued pacing.

Lucy watched this play out, her mind elsewhere in a haze. Confused, she looked to her side where she still saw her handbag, resting on the bench beside her.

Strange...

A bus stopped by. The door opened with a mechanical hiss. Then it closed when she didn't board, and moved on, driving past the thief who lay motionless on the pavement. The hero stood up, breathing a little heavy, holding Lucy's handbag...

Some pedestrian applauded.

Lucy got up to leave.

"Here you go ma'am." The hero chased after her.

Not responding, Lucy looked to the bench—nope, the bag wasn't there. She grasped it from the Handbag Hero and started heading home.

"Are you okay?" the man called after her, but didn't follow.

On autopilot, Lucy checked her mail when she got to the apartment building. She tossed out the junk, keeping only one specific letter that she frowned at.

- Chapter Two -
"Reunion"

Mary's house was very orderly. She never thought she'd miss how messy it could get. She sighed at a family photo where Frank held baby Lucy at the park. Looking longingly in his eyes, so full of life in that photo, she sighed as if he could hear her thoughts now.

When Lucy moved out, she thought the place would feel empty. But she'd speak to Frank quite often. She wasn't quite as advanced as her daughter, so Frank never responded.

She did what everyone did after they lost someone and wanted to feel close to them. And she ended up discovering that at age fifty-six, it was quite a blessing to live on her own, completely in charge of her house. Her only daughter was a blessing in her own right, and Mary was proud of the progress she'd made. But now, Mary got to be herself. A new self that she hadn't known while she was a mother, worrying about Lucy's mental health all the time.

Finally, Lucy was better. Such a relief. So much so that she'd had time to hang up a few more pictures on the walls in the hallways, fill jars with homemade pickles, arrange flowers in vases. In fact, it was a little busy, though not a clutter by any means.

At the moment, she was busy chopping parsley when someone knocked firmly. Rinsing her hands, Mary hurried along, wiping them on her apron. She checked through the peephole then swung the door open.

"Knocking like it's the bloody coppers..." No one was there. She expected to find a package delivered. Instead, she saw a scrunched-up letter on her front step. Unfurling it, Mary read the good news, an approval for a premises license to sell alcohol.

"Lucy...?"

Looking up, she didn't see her daughter anywhere. Something was wrong. Mary grabbed her cell and called.

*

Léon the plant almost looked sad when Lucy brushed past without a care, dropping her handbag as she entered. Inside, her phone buzzed lightly. *'Mum'* was calling. Lucy disconnected. Four missed calls. She sent her mother a message. If she wouldn't respond, the woman would be on her front step—Lucy didn't have the emotional capacity to deal with that right now.

Moving to her vision board, she mulled over the way she'd mapped out her life in an orderly fashion. Graduating high school, moving into a new house with her own family. The later portions weren't ticked off like some of the earlier ones, one of which was weaning off citalopram, an antidepressant. Lucy eyed the big heading: *13 Years Free.*

"One year, eh?" Lingering there for a moment, anger bubbled up within. Unimaginable rage and despair. She'd been cheated. "Not enough for *this*... or *this*... or *that*..."

One by one she pulled off portions of her board from the future of the timeline.

An apiary.

Wooden aging barrels.

A wedding dress.

One picture in particular made Lucy pause; a silhouetted couple watching the sunset from a hill. Her teenage self made this one. The glittery "fall in love" caption was so stupid.

For the first time since she got the terrible news, she broke into a sobbing fit. When did this even happen? She'd been doing all the right things, followed every step to turn her life into the best version it could be despite her challenges, and then those challenges came and bit her in the arse to spite her. Life wasn't a bitch; it was downright cruel. Throat closing up, vision blurring, it just ticked her off more, because every minute that passed made this all the more real. She didn't know who to hate more in that moment, her mother or Dr Gray. In this whirlwind, she suddenly felt sorry for her mother, who'd only ever tried to help. It was *them*—only their fault.

Clamouring into the bathroom, Lucy scooped her medications out of the medicine cabinet. St John's wort and clozapine. Opening the window in her living room, she poured the pills into her palms and flung them out, screaming.

Someone yelled at her from one below, "Oy! Keep it down! People trying to sleep here!"

Lucy fumed, "Shut the fuck up you stupid twat!"

"I'll call the coppers you freak!"

"Bugger off!" Chucking out the empty bottles, Lucy tried to hit the complaining tenant's window. She didn't see if she missed or not, and didn't really care. Slamming her pane shut, the tiniest of cracks appeared in the corner.

Heaving as if she'd run up six flights of stairs, Lucy felt just a little lighter. She was a whole lot more tired than she had been. Ever. Exhausted to the point of no return. She briefly wondered if that's what dying would feel like. Maybe it wouldn't be so bad.

Peeking through the drawn curtain, the first rays of light shone on Lucy's face. On the couch, she woke, sniffed. Checking her buzzing phone, she saw a missed call from work.

In her stained pajamas, she surveyed the fridge. No food. When was the last time she'd gone grocery shopping? From the empty Pyrex containers and glass jars piled in the sink, it had been a while. Lucy found a half-empty tub of ice cream in the back of her freezer and grabbed a spoon.

A copy of Bram Stoker's *Dracula* was mounted on the little stand next to her plant. Lucy plopped the book on the floor and sat on it, digging into the ice cream.

"Who's going to take care of you now, Léon?" she asked the leafy green. Her eyes swelled up again. She blinked it away, glancing at the friendly pot plant. Lucy buried her head in her knees, still exhausted after another full night's sleep.

Someone called her. It sounded like Lucy, yet in contrast, this voice had an American accent. "When are you going to call your mom?" she asked.

Lucy ignored it. Waited. Although she hoped it would go away, she knew it wouldn't. She hadn't been taking any meds, eating terribly. They hadn't been back in years. Not once. Only slight, unrelated visions. It seemed momentous enough to come back now more than ever.

"Lucy?" the voice pressed. "You've got to tell her."

Another chimed in, this one with an Australian accent. "Come on Luce, leave her alone," it said dismissively. "She doesn't want to talk to us. Besides, it's her mum's fault we're in this mess!"

"But it's been so long—we have to be here for her now more than ever—it's *Lucy* for heaven's sake!" American Luce retorted.

"She wants nothing to do with us—"

A British voice interrupted the Australian. "Serves her right!" This one sounded *exactly* like Lucy. And she was acidic.

Lucy still sat there, not reacting. Maybe they'd just argue amongst themselves and give it up after a bit. Wishful thinking.

"Took those bloody meds to shut us out," the third voice went on, "buried us in the ground, and now...let her die alone."

"Lucifera..." American Luce said, "that wasn't her choice."

"She's a grown woman!" Lucifera shouted.

The voices whispered to each other, unintelligible. It turned into a ruckus inside Lucy's skull. She knew what she had to do.

Lucy filled up a bath. Humming, *"Everything for love..."*

Lu, the Australian, spoke up, "Oh I love this song! Haven't heard it in ages..."

"The clip scared the hell out of me," Luce said.

Lu giggled, "You're such a sissy."

"Shut up, bitch," said Luce. "You're scared of spiders."

"Have you seen the size of the spiders where I come from?" Lu shot back in her Australian drawl.

"Oh, you mean... Lucy's head?" Luce asked, sounding pleased with her witty retort.

It took forever for the bath to fill. Lucy sank in a rush, fully dressed. The cold shock was welcome as she slid under the surface, leaving only her mouth and nose out for air.

Silence at last.

After a few deep breaths she popped her head out. The silence continued. Grateful for this small reprieve, she opened her eyes.

Lucy sighed in frustration as Lucinda entered the bathroom. She was Lucy's Celtic witch doppelgänger. Frizzy red hair, heavy Irish accent. She wore a tight, flowing black dress with sleeves drooping just a little past her wrists like leaves.

Lucinda smiled, "Long time no see, lass."

For the first time, Lucy reciprocated. "You were gone for so bloody long."

"Not the hello I was expecting. Then again, you did bury us alive."

"I can't do this again..."

"Boohoo," Lucinda mocked.

"You filling in for Lucifera?"

"The two of you have a lot of shite to work out between yourselves." She sat on the closed toilet, crossing her legs as if it were a chair in a dining hall.

"She going to make an appearance too?" Lucy asked, a little nervous about that interaction.

"I'm a Celtic witch, Lucy, not a seer," Lucinda said.

The others, Lu and Luce, didn't usually come in physical form, just tagged along as voices. Though Lucy did see them once in a while. Lucifera and Lucinda were the ones that usually showed themselves in her 'realm.'

"Can you please just give me some space? Peace of mind?"

"I think I've let you wallow long enough," Lucinda said.

"So, you were watching, eh?" Lucy sneered. "Is that it? Now you're back to make what's left as awful as possible?"

Her Celtic counterpart appeared genuinely offended. "You know damn well I would never do that. I hate seeing you like this."

Lucinda's eyes were deep emerald unlike Lucy's brown. In that instance she felt something small and comforting that she hadn't experienced in a while. She knew, as she always did, that she could trust Lucinda. Even after the extensive measures she'd gone through to shut her out.

"I'm still a part of you," she said. Bending down by the bathtub, Lucinda was solemn yet assertive. "Look, there's one last thing you have to do. Before we go."

Lucy chuckled mirthlessly. "You mean before I die?"

"You have to live," Lucinda said.

Lucy didn't feel frustration or anger at that; it was a different emotional string that Lucinda just plucked. Not wanting to go down that path, she tried to brush it off. "This is insane. I shouldn't have thrown my meds out the window."

"And where did your medicine get you?" Lucinda watched her closely. She was always the level-headed one.

Lucy pondered. She didn't know how to feel about this. She'd always missed Lucinda. Wished she could just have her without Lucifera as part of the package deal...but that was never a reality.

"You've been eating and sleeping your life away since you got the news," Lucinda took Lucy's hand in hers.

God, it felt like real human touch. Warm.

"What would you have me do?" Lucy asked despite herself.

"You've always wanted to open a meadery in Ireland," Lucinda said. "Do it!"

A beat. Was Lucy actually considering this? She shook her head, quickly, taking her hand back into the cold bath water. It was really starting to get to her now, gnawing at her bones.

"This is insane! Open a meadery? Just like that?"

Lucy splashed out the bathtub. In the mirror, Lucifera glowered at her as she walked out. She didn't pay attention.

Lucinda followed.

Lucy pushed her wet hair back in frustration. Shivering. "Stop following me, Lucinda!" she entered her bedroom.

Off the floor, Lucinda plucked a crumpled piece of paper with a two-storey building. Looked like it was from the Middle Ages. "You've been eyeing this place a while now. Why not?"

Lucy scoffed at her.

"You've got the licenses you need."

"I'm dying! There's no time!

Lucinda stomped a foot on the ground, making fists. "What have you got to lose, lass?"

Lucy opened her mouth to give a long, detailed answer of exactly everything she had to lose, but she couldn't. Not now, in this state. Looming death made things a lot clearer. Lying to yourself seemed like a waste. And still it was tough for her to admit that she'd wasted every living moment being "normal".

"Money? You won't be needing that. Security? Stability—that's all gone out the window—your grumpy neighbour down there got the last of it." She raised her eyebrows.

This actually made Lucy think about it seriously. But no..."I can't just up and go."

"Why?" Lucinda pressed, coming right up to her. She was wearing Lucy's favourite perfume. Light, tasteful. Wistful. "Is it your Mum?"

Something flashed over Lucy. Wouldn't she have done the same thing if their roles were reversed? Lucy always told herself she would have taken her own daughter to Dr Gray. It didn't matter. None of it mattered. It was what it was, and she couldn't change the past. She'd spent years being angry at her mother and still doing what she said and now...

"Just call her from Ireland," Lucinda shrugged.

No, she shouldn't do that to Mary, "It'll worry her to death."

"I love Mary, and I know she cares for you," Lucinda said. "But she will be fine. Now is not the time to live for someone else, Lucy."

Grappling with the idea, Lucy felt like a little girl who might be plucking petals off a flower. She stared at her Celtic self.

Lu spoke up. It always sounded like it came from outside, like she and Luce were voice over artists in Lucy's personal reality show.

"You're dying." Lu was blunt as ever. "Why not?"

"I suppose there's nothing to lose..." Luce said tentatively.

"Live before I die, " Lucy mumbled. "Nothing to lose, eh?"

"Only time." Lucinda watched her intently. Anxious.

"She's gonna do it!" Luce whispered with the same nervous excitement that was simmering in Lucy's core.

"No, she won't," Lu chided.

"She is!"

"She doesn't have the balls!"

"Yes..."

"Does she?"

"Nothing to lose..." Lucy repeated slowly.

The voices hushed completely.

After a short few seconds, Luce's light whisper came, "Is that a yes?"

"Shh!" Lucinda hissed.

Lucy breathed in, just like she did in the bath when she wanted to shut them all up.

A heartbeat.

"Screw it," Lucy said.

"Yes!" Lucinda shook a victorious fist in the air.

"All in, balls out!" Lu cheered.

Lucy chuckled a little. She was nervous as ever, but she was free in a whole new, different way she'd never felt before. And that was more exciting than anything on earth.

- Chapter Three -
"Bánánach"

The hallway outside was quiet. No street noise or chatter made it through. Mary knocked on Lucy's door, edgy as ever. She had no patience to wait for a response before trying again.

"Lucy?" She pressed her lips close to the door, hoping to be heard. "Lucy, it's Mum. Open up. Come on, you can't stay cooped up in there forever."

Immediately regretting that last statement, Mary cringed. She knew how her daughter thought, why would she say that after the terrible news she'd gotten? But there had to be other options. She wouldn't let her waste away here. There was always another way, and she'd given Lucy enough time to wallow. A week was too much. Now it was time to move on and look forward.

Another knock. More aggressive. Still nothing. Mary chose her words carefully, softened her voice. "Lucy, I miss you. I know it's hard now but can you just let me in? We don't even have to talk. I'll cook something nice and..." After giving it a few more seconds, Mary rummaged in her purse for a set of keys. She unlocked Lucy's door, pulled down the handle.

Upon seeing the door chain hanging loose on the frame, Mary eased it open fully to find a sink full of dishes. Curtains all drawn shut.

"Lucy?" she checked again.

After surveying the messy bedroom, Mary returned to open the windows in the rest of the house. By the TV, she noticed a small envelope with *"Mum"* scribbled on it in almost illegible handwriting. Curious, uneasy, she opened the letter; a DVD titled *"Play Me."* Tentative, Mary did.

Awkward smile, Lucy appeared onscreen. Waved at the camera. "Hi Mum."

"Oh, hell's bells what is this?" Mary mumbled, glued to the TV.

"I decided to leave a video message instead of a letter because...you know my handwriting," Lucy glanced aside briefly. "Anyway, if you're watching this..."

Mary smacked both hands over her mouth, shocked to the core, scared to hear the next words.

"...then I'm already off on my little adventure," Lucy said cheerily, glancing aside again. "I just needed some time alone to clear my head from all the—you know. Sorry I didn't call. Anyway, let's do a video chat on Sunday."

Only now Mary sighed in relief, still rather irate at the unnecessary scare.

"No need to worry about me," Lucy went on, "I'm totally safe. Oh—and can you please take care of Léon until I'm back? His mister is next to him. Thanks Mum." She blew a kiss, reached for the camera. "Love you." The video cut out.

Mary fumbled for words. She had to say something, she couldn't just accept this, it was outrageous! The recording was over and she was agitated and confounded, but what could she do except wait?

At the door, she stopped by the Chinese evergreen. "I suppose this is Léon..." She scooped up the plant with the accompanying mister and exited. She found herself missing her late husband now more than ever. He would have been able to get through to Lucy.

*

Baggy-eyed, exhausted, travelling light as an air hostess, Lucy stood at the airport's entrance staring at the taxis parked just outside. As she walked up to one of them, Lucinda trailed behind, beaming. The Celtic witch was home at last.

Dublin, Ireland.

The taxi driver, a man in his sixties, smiled at the rearview mirror. Lucinda sat in the back seat with Lucy. It felt strangely nostalgic to have someone next to her that others couldn't see, her own little secret, like having superpowers. She remembered liking that feeling when she was younger. . He spoke in a foreign accent.

"So, where are we visiting, from?" he asked.

"Where is *he* from?" Lucinda asked.

"From—" Lucy started, but he cut in with excitement.

"Wait, wait! No say anything. I'm guess... say something."

"You don't sound Irish," Lucy played along.

"England!" he said.

"You got it."

"I knew it!" he laughed, taking a left turn at an intersection. "I'm Romanian. But my wife is Irish. I teached her to eat good food. She teached me how to drink."

While he found his joke amusing, Lucinda glared at the plump man. Lucy was unenthusiastic about the conversation, just nodding politely at this point. She sent a quick text message to someone she'd labelled 'Cunningham Estate Agent.' *In Dublin. See you at the hotel this evening,* Lucy typed.

"You know," the driver was still rambling as talkative taxi drivers did. "I love the monarchy in England. They take care of country. In Romania, where I'm from...*argh!* It's not like it used to be." He shook his head morosely.

Lucy frowned. "You mean, communism?"

"Now there's no money, people hungry, hard to find job."

"You know England's not communist, right?"

"Yes, but it's same."

Lucy had no idea how to react, so she didn't. Instead, she looked out the window, watching the sights. A few old buildings. A horse galloping through the street at full speed. She pointed to it, wanting to comment, but the driver didn't seem to have noticed, so she let it go. Maybe it was there, maybe not.

Her cell *dinged* with a response from the estate agent: *Welcome! Looking forward to meeting you in person. You're going to love the place.* Sending a reply, Lucy smiled to herself, starting to feel that holiday vibe setting in.

Upon arriving at the Cleland Castle Retreat, Lucy was about to pay the taxi driver the price on the meter.

"Du-te in pizdamatii!" he mumbled in Romanian, pissed off suddenly.

"What? The meter—"

"Out! Out!" he waved, refusing to meet Lucy's eyes as he angrily got out himself and popped open the boot, standing there, tapping his foot impatiently.

Scoffing at him, Lucy grabbed her bag. "Well, I'm definitely not giving you a tip now…" She tried handing him the money again.

"No, no, no, no, no." Refusing the cash, he got back in the car and revved off.

Beside Lucy, Lucinda raised her eyebrows. "Gobshite commie."

"Figures," Lucy mumbled. Though a bad mood couldn't last. Lucy looked up at the place. An actual castle. Turrets, parapets and all, surrounded by exquisite lawns and lively trees.

Moss and vines spread along half the face of the structure, having been trimmed to reveal some windows. It was a sight to behold, and Lucy loved it. The inside did not disappoint with high ceilings and chandeliers. Clean and immaculate. Impressive to say the least. Lucy made her way to the front desk, no longer accompanied by Lucinda. She came and left as she pleased. Not always visible, yet always there.

A bored clerk greeted her with a fake smile. "Can I help you ma'am?"

"Not at the moment, thanks," Lucy said, "I'm waiting to meet someone." She didn't want to start the checking in process when she had a meeting coming up in a few minutes. She'd do it all afterwards.

"Mh-hm," the bored guy deigned another cold smile and walked off.

Lucy took a seat. A few moments passed. She pulled out her copy of Bram Stoker's *Dracula*. If there was a right time and place to read one of her favourite books her father had gotten her hooked on, this was it. Only that this time, the novel acted as a sleeping pill.

"Ma'am?" She jerked awake. The bored clerk stood over her.

"Is she here?" Lucy asked, wiping her eyes.

"Who?"

Lucy glanced out the window, the sun halfway gone. "The estate agent. Did someone come in?"

"Nobody came in looking for you."

"You sure? 'Cause I—"

"Trust me ma'am, it was hard to miss you. You snored quite loudly," he gave her an icy smile, "perhaps I could show you a room now?"

"All right," Lucy nodded. Already she was having some doubts about this. If this agent didn't show up to the meeting, how reliable was she?

The clerk led Lucy up a winding staircase worthy of a castle. The curves in the wood of the bannister had an almost hypnotizing design.

Shown around the room, the bathroom was equipped with a fancy clawfoot tub and built-in wardrobes. The view from the room was magnificent, open fields surrounding the area.

"This is really nice," she said.

The bored guy nodded.

"I'll take it."

For an instant, his smile flickered to an angry frown, brows furrowed, chin low. darkened with shadows.

Once she was back up there alone with her suitcase, Lucy's eyes landed on the double bed. "This'll do." She threw herself on the mattress. And...she was out.

Blanket in a mess, Lucy was flat faced on the bed, lying diagonally, drooling on the pillow, when Lucinda shook her.

"Ho! Lucy! Wake up!" she urged, sitting on the bedside table.

Lucy cracked her eyes open slowly, "My head's bursting..."

"Something you've got to do, lass." Lucinda was far too animated for this hour.

"Not now, Lucinda." Lucy turned over to the other side. She rolled out of bed against her will—the entire room tilted, angled to the side. Bed, side tables, chairs, everything was anchored to the spot except Lucy.

"What the hell?" She tried to get her bearings.

"Welcome to the Otherworld," Lucinda uttered in an overly witchy voice.

Lucy tried to stand, lost balance, so she stayed on her knees. "What is this?"

"Death looming upon you," Lucinda chanted. "The banshee has keened. The Otherworld awaits. A *bánánach* searches for you, Lucy."

As Lucy crawled around the bed, Lucinda followed, though she had no problem walking on the tilted ground. Lucy looked up at her from her crouched position, scoffed.

"You have to capture it," the witch explained.

"A banana?"

"*Bánánach!*" Lucinda corrected. "She's a demon. Drawn to the stench of death."

"Wonderful..." Lucy really didn't feel like this nonsense now. But from experience, when her episodes took a hold so prominently, they wouldn't rest until she faced them fully. And she was stupid enough to fling her meds out the window. Now she was paying the price. Yup, Lucy deserved this. Hopefully she could get it over with quickly and just get back to bed without any nonsense acting up until morning. She pinched herself just to make sure.

"You're awake, Lucy!" Lucinda sounded annoyed. "It's downstairs."

Pissed off, Lucy blinked hard through the horrible combination of vertigo and headache. "Seriously?"

The room tilted violently. In this insane haze, Lucy headed for the door, which angled away from her on an incline.

She dragged herself out past one of her messy, open suitcases. Lucinda pointed to a nearly-empty glass bottle.

"You'll need that to capture—"

"The banana demon, got it," Lucy said curtly, head still throbbing. She drank the last sip of water.

It was a mission, but she managed to climb out the room. Crawling along the floor, Lucy made her way to a large arched opening. "This is *ridiculous*... I can't stand."

"The Otherworld is spiritual; your legs are physical. It'll get easier after your first time."

"That's what she said..." Lu's voice came from somewhere.

Lucy groaned indignantly. She gripped the first velvety step of the staircase. Figures in oil paintings on the wall shifted and blurred like a kaleidoscope. Lucy managed to stabilize herself on the bannister.

By the second landing, someone else stepped onto the stairs. The whole building was wobbly, while she shrank closer to the railing. Glued to her phone, this other hotel guest didn't seem to notice Lucy at first but jumped at the sight when she did.

Even though she was having a full-blown episode, out of control, Lucy was still lucid enough to understand what the other person must be seeing...a well-lit staircase with a huddled Lucy clinging to the bannister like it's the Titanic's bulwark.

The Hotel Guest gave an awkward nod, keeping her distance from Lucy.

On the other hand, Lucy saw something otherworldly. A woman's body with a beastly head. A flickering image, glowing vaguely in half-light. Features a dark mess of lines with hollow black eyes and a crow's skull. She waited for the creature-lady to pad a wide, tentative circle around her, get out of sight.

"It's not real..." she told herself over and over again, "It's not real..."

Lucifera's voice came then, disembodied, *"She's not cut out for this,"* she sneered.

"Where have you been!?" American Luce answered her.

"She can't do it," Lucifera said haughtily.

Australian Lu drawled, *"You think she'll give up?"*

"She can't give up! She has to push through—" American Luce persisted.

"*What's a banana demon anyway?*" Lu sounded skeptical. "*I think Lucifera's just messing with us.*"

"*She'll die alone,*" Lucifera said coldly.

"Everyone dies alone," Lucy grumbled as she ploughed on.

Their voices blended into rushed whispers.

At the lobby, the white tiled floor was speckled with black, blinking crow eyes. Lucy heard laughter, her own voice, coming from outside. Distant, it faded away quickly.

Not a single soul was down here—save for one. A man on a lobby couch, asleep, leaning back on the rest with his mouth half open. The rest was Lucy's brain going haywire. No matter how many times she told herself this was only in her head, it felt more real than anything. There was logic, there was heart. And now she was scared of what she saw. Just because there was so much unknown waiting for her at the other side of this, once it was all over, after a year. She had no idea what to expect. That was terrifying. Even more terrifying than the translucent humanoid figure towered above the sleeping guy. Hovering. It had the vague form of a woman, holding both sides of the man's head, leaning down.

The creature's nails were bloody long and sharp. She was shimmering in and out of focus, like shards of glass convulsing in the low light. The *Bánánach* bent lower, sounding a horrible hiss as she brought her open mouth closer to the dozing man's, like she was going to kiss him.

Blinking hard, Lucy tried to snap out of the haze. "God, I wish I had my meds."

The *Bánánach* whipped around. Her black hair moved sluggishly as if she were under water. Screeching like a banshee, the demon's jaw dropped lower, her form flickering more rapidly.

Behind Lucy, Lucinda urged her on, "Repeat after me!"

The creature glided to Lucy, who opened the empty bottle and pointed it at her. She tensed up, thrown into her very own horror film in the most surreally real experience she'd had in thirteen years, and by far the worst.

She repeated Lucinda's foreign words religiously, *"Chan annleatsa a tha mi!"*

The *bánánach* shrieked as she was sucked into the bottle in a swirl of shadows. Lucy breathed in relief. Felt the bottle shake in her hand a little as she sealed the cap with urgency. This was insane. Absolutely bonkers. And now that it was over, the high of the rush was actually quite enjoyable. She hoped her brain wouldn't discern that as a signal for more of these wild episodes. She didn't even know how this all worked.

With the flutter of an eyelid, everything around Lucy melted back to normal. The crow eyes on the white floor were simply smaller black tiles. She tightened the bottle cap, the undulating blackness inside now gone. Even so, she'd never dare open that thing.

Tired as hell with dizziness befitting a hangover, Lucy slumped on the couch across from the man. She hadn't noticed he was awake, watching her.

"Chonaícméthú ag breathnúorm," he grinned.

Lucy looked up at him. Lucinda sat beside him, leaning close, staring at him with a mesmerised smile. He was tall and rugged, with a short beard, and hair in a Viking-worthy ponytail behind his head.

"Huh?"

"Chonaícméthú ag breathnúorm," he repeated.

"I don't speak Irish," Lucy said.

"Means he 'saw you looking,'" Lucinda translated.

Lucy frowned at that. Odd...

The guy switched to English, with a notable Irish accent. "Sorry...I could have sworn I heard you mumbling in Gaeilge before."

"Oh...I...took it in school once," she dismissed, "Sometimes I mumble weird things."

"I talk to myself too," he laughed lightly. "I like your outfit. Bold."

Lucy looked down at her cartoon kitten pajamas. "Oh that...yeah..."

"Must have been quite the party."

"Huh?"

"You look wasted," he said.

Lucy almost giggled at how ridiculous Lucinda appeared on the same couch as him, still staring, star-struck. Her right side wasn't her best side. And Lucy found herself subconsciously turning her own head a little.

"Yeah. I better get going."

Lucinda's jaw dropped, while Lucifera's voice filled the air with her trademark sneering laugh.

"Hello?" the stranger waved at her. Apparently he said something, and she hadn't quite paid attention.

"What?"

"I was asking what you've got in your bottle?"

"Air... I suppose." What else could she say?

He laughed, "I do that too."

"Trap air?"

"Aye. Well, have a look." Unzipping a bag at his feet, he extracted a roll-up pouch. Unfolded, it revealed an array of small, corked glass jars. All empty.

Lucy leaned forward a little to get a good look at the labels.

"Pretty neat, ain't it?" he asked.

"Australia, South Africa, Romania..." Now she understood, smirking, "I get it...you're trapping air from different countries as a souvenir."

"I know it's dumb, but it means something to me." He shrugged. "And I see you're inclined to doing the same."

"Did you just call me dumb?" She waved the glass bottle with a smile. This conversation was taking a weirder turn than her previous visions. But it was more fun and refreshing than the banana demon. At least she might not have nightmares tonight after ending on a more positive note with a nice stranger she'd never see again.

He chuckled again, clearly not knowing what to make of her, but interested nonetheless. Lucinda had gone from the couch now. It was only Lucy and the Irishman. Neither of them said anything for a beat. Lucy straightened up, ready to leave.

"Well, I'll..." she pointed back toward the stairs.

"Before you go," he stood as well, pulling out a glass vial labelled *Ireland*. He uncorked it, waved it around.

Lucy couldn't help giggling at the sight. He looked ridiculous.

"Shazam!" she joked.

"Just wanted to 'capture' this moment." He sealed the vial carefully.

"What's so important about this moment?"

"I don't know yet. Just know it is."

The shadow of a smile flashed on Lucy's lips.

"Anyway...*oidhchemhath*," he said.

"Good night?" Lucy guessed.

"You're good." He held out his hand. "I'm Matt by the way."

"Lucinda—Lucy," she never really used her full name. Probably got mixed up now because the Celtic witch wouldn't stop staring when she was on the couch before.

Lucy walked off. Again, Lucinda was beside her, walking backwards, looking at Matt, waving her hands. "You know what he's thinking right now?"

"Hmm?" Lucy kept walking ahead.

"What, you can read thoughts now?" Luce's voice asked sincerely.

"Idiot..." Lu retorted.

"He's thinking..." Lucinda took back the mic, put on a deep voice, "I hate to see you go, but I love to watch you leave." She gasped, "Is that a smile I see on your face, Lucy?"

"Oh, she's smitten," Luce added.

"Shut up," Lucy told them. "I'm never going to see him again. Still, it's nice to be reminded I'm such a catch even in my cat-lady pajamas when I'm hunting banana demons with glass bottles."

The voices in her head giggled. Lucy turned the corner. Started climbing the stairs. That same woman that came down before walked into the hallway with a small packet in hand. Noticing Lucy, she halted in her tracks and made a U-turn.

Lucy threw a glance. "What's wrong with her?"

Dismissively, Lucinda rolled her eyes, shaking her head. "Lots of weirdos out there..."

The two of them made their way up. Lucy's step was just a little lighter than it had been lately.

- Chapter Four -
"Signed in Blood"

Leaves rustle on the vines of the creepers that mask the face of the magnificent building. Wild but tamed. Fluttering with a throaty squawk, the crow lands atop a nearby tree. It picks behind its wing a bit, takes off again, going high up, around the hotel. Wind swirls noisily.

Lucy pulled the plug of the clawfoot tub, letting the water drain. She wrapped a towel around her hair, and didn't take any pills.

The taxi pulled up in front of a humble single-storey building. Stone-faced, built like a castle—new but made to look old. Nestled spaciously between two similarly old-fashioned structures; to the right, there was a vintage guitar store. To the left, a clothing shop.

Steel rods held up a *For Sale* sign in the front garden of Castle Brewery. That's all that greeted Lucy when she got there.

"Leave the metre running, yeah?" she asked the driver.

She pulled a crumpled paper from her pocket, held up the image of the place from her vision board. Lucinda looked over her shoulder.

"Same place..." murmured Lucy.

"Well, where is that woman?" asked Lucinda.

"Said she'd be here at two." Lucy checked her phone. *14:02.*

"It looks lovely."

Large off-white stones, an angled, red-tiled roof, cottage windows, arched entrance doors that Lucy tried, though they were locked. She circled the building to where she could hop over a low fence. Someone smoking a pipe at the music store gave her a friendly wave, which she returned.

The backyard had a small Wendy house. Old, mouldy, unused.

"We'll have to get rid of that." Lucy was already forgetting she didn't have more than a year. She was seeing far into the future, where her dream was running for a long time. But if dying was like falling asleep, maybe she could carry on dreaming forever.

"There's a lot of space," Lucinda said.

The others never seemed to know what Lucy was thinking. No more than any other person outside her head might guess through expressions and body language. That was one thing that she always appreciated, no matter how bad things got with her visions, no matter what arguments she had with these fragments of herself, she always had total privacy inside her own thoughts.

Lucy padded along, envisioning the meadery. "Could set up a nice pergola over here. Hang some lights."

"Torches on the side." Lucinda's eyes twinkled. "Or sconces!"

"No... Just old-fashioned street lamps" Lucy pointed to the spots where she'd want them. "Two over here. A few barrels for good taste."

As Lucy described what she'd do with the place, someone else joined them. Matt, from the hotel. He beamed when he saw her.

"You? What are you doing here?" Lucy was astounded.

"You're my two o'clock?" Matt asked.

"You can't be serious..." This was way too much of a coincidence.

Matt laughed and handed a folder to Lucy. She saw his face on the business card inside. *Matthew Cunningham, Estate Agent.*

Lucinda was ecstatic.

"Matthew Cunningham... Matt...what are the odds? I thought I was meeting a lady."

"She just makes the appointments." He seemed very pleased at this turn of events.

"You don't look like an estate agent."

"What does an estate agent look like?"

"Not a Viking."

"I'll take that as a compliment." He held up the keys. "Shall I show you around?"

Lucinda was gone from view. Lucy closed the file and followed.

Two old, stainless-steel fermenters guarded a bare wall behind the wooden counter. Rafters jutted along the top, giving the place a real rustic feel. The floor was tiled, all open-plan and echoing as Matt showed Lucy around.

"Place used to be a brewery. The previous owner moved to a bigger spot closer to the city hubbub."

"Yeah, McCormack told me. I've been eyeing this spot for a few months. I'm surprised no one's snatched it."

"What do you plan on doing with it?"

"Meadery," she said.

"Meadery? You mean making...mead?"

"Yeah." She grinned at his confusion.

"What *is* mead?" he asked finally. "I've heard it mentioned in fantasy stories."

"What kind of Viking are you?"

Matt laughed, "An Irish one,"

"It's the oldest alcoholic beverage known to man. Fermented honey water."

"Huh...cool. And you know how to make this?"

"Yeah."

"So, you're expanding your business from England?" he guessed, "I presume that's where you're from."

"No and yes." Lucy looked into one of the rooms that had a few empty old crates in it. "I don't brew for a living. I'm an accountant."

"Nah," he said. "You don't look like an accountant."

"What does an accountant look like?"

"Boring. And not..." He trailed off, but she knew what he was going to say. "Well, I stand corrected. You're living proof!" Matt's laughter boomed.

After the tour, Lucy waited outside the front entrance for Matt to lock the doors. "So, what do you think?"

"I'll sleep on it."

"Sounds like a plan." He glanced over at the guitar shop next door. "Your taxi?" he asked.

"Yeah."

"All right. I'll see you around. Give me a call." He winked jokingly. Lucy chuckled as she got into the car. Matt headed to the music store. That same guy smoking a pipe greeted him as he approached.

As she got in the taxi, Lucy watched him. She was looking forward to seeing him again the next time.

Asleep, in front of the TV in the lounge area, the woman is totally oblivious to the fact that it's daytime despite the sun shining on her face through the open curtain. It seems silent and peaceful in there.

The black bird flies at full speed toward the window, a miscalculation—it smacks into the pane—

Lucy jolted upright at a loud noise. Rubbing sleep out her eyes, she stared at the window where the glass was cracked. A red smudge smeared where a crow had crashed.

"What the hell...?" Barefoot, Lucy approached it, peering outside at the dark creature in a jumble of feathers, spasming twice more before going limp. "Poor thing..." She felt awful for it, must have just seen something interesting beyond the glass that was evidently too clean for avian safety.

A loud winching noise made Lucy whip around in fright. Something was different. Off. Way off...

She was still in her room. She could see the bed, the couch, the door.

There were also trees in here.

Looking up, grey skies, more crows fluttering. She immediately turned back to the window, and the dead crow was still there. So that one was real.

Tombstones stood erect before her. Lucy curled her toes into the moist grass. She recognised this place. A snippet of Brompton Cemetery, where they buried her father when she was only seven years old. But this wasn't her father's funeral.

A pine box was being lowered into a dark gaping maw in the earth. No visitors paying their respects. Just Lucy, her mother, Mary, and Dr Gray standing behind her— behind her teen self—whose gaze was also glued to the coffin. A new character she'd never seen before was also present. A gravedigger. A towering, muscular beast with a ram's head. Humanoid. Shirtless. Shovel in his fist.

On the other end of the burial stood teen Lucifera. Neither she nor the younger Lucy paid the present-day Lucy any attention. Lucifera, the spitting image of herself, made eye contact with teen Lucy. She bit her jaw, all sorrow, dying on the inside. The girl shook her head slowly.

Teen Lucy's lip quivered. The Gravedigger began shovelling from a mound of pink, white and yellow pills into the grave. The beast snorted slightly as it worked. Millions of meds clattered hollowly on the wood.

While the younger version of herself was averted to the ground, Lucy saw that teen Lucifera was being totally ignored in her pain. The young doppelgänger wiped tears from her red eyes, turned and shuffled away deeper into the hotel room, disappearing behind a large gravestone.

A mere observer on the sidelines of this memory, Lucy wiped her eyes. The scene was still there. Still visible, trees and all. The gravedigger snorted as he worked. Closing her eyes, Lucy inhaled slowly, and dared another glance as she breathed out.

*

Driving, Mary was on her phone, reaching Lucy's voicemail again. "Oh, not again!" She disconnected the call. Redialed. Voicemail again. This time she left a message. "Lucy! You better listen to this voicemail young lady! I'm on my way to the police, I'm reporting you missing!" She choked up a bit, "I swear, just—" She paused to get a handle on herself. "Just answer me dear—please answer me—I don't know what's gotten into you."

She hung up, then tried yet again. While it rang, her cell dinged. Tapping the screen impatiently, she opened the message, half an eye on the red light as she read it.

Can't talk now Mum, call you back later <3

"Oh, thank God." The phone rang. "Lucy!?" Someone behind hooted impatiently. Mary hit the accelerator. "No, Clint, I can't. Will you just show the house?" A retort she didn't care for, "I—then ask Beverly!"

Flashing lights reflected in the rear-view mirror. "Oh bollocks!" She indicated and pulled over.

*

A green vista overlooked the expanse of a golf course, all visible from the Peak Terrace of the Cleland Castle's Clubhouse. A lovely morning. A few quiet conversations buzzed in the background. Not many people were here.

Alone at a table, Lucy browsed a menu. Someone hovered above her.

"Oh, that was quick."

It wasn't the waitress, but the estate agent. "Morning, Lucy."

"Good morning, Michael," she said.

Lucinda echoed with an urgent correction to '*Matt*'.

"Matt!" Lucy added quickly, "Good morning, *Matt*."

"May I join you?" He'd come here to meet her about the brewery, but he was still being a gentleman. How refreshing.

Lucy gestured to the chair across, and Matt took it. In the subtext of the little banter that didn't matter, Lucy couldn't stop thinking how unfortunate it was that she wasn't going to stay for too long. She couldn't get into anything. Besides, who got into something after two meetings? She was way ahead of herself. Living before she died had become her motto of late, but she couldn't exactly apply that to everything. She veered herself out of that mindset. Nevertheless, there was no problem in a bit of harmless flirtatiousness.

"So, what do you think of Ireland so far?" he asked.

"Haven't gotten a chance to see much of it yet."

"Oh, you're going to love it. When I first came here, I couldn't get enough of the castles."

"You're not from here?"

"Half Scottish. Lived there for my formative years."

"Oh wow. Castles you say?"

"Oh yes."

"Loads of history in those walls," Lucy said thoughtfully.

"No, I like it for the sheer pleasure of real estate." He grinned.

Lucy gave a small, polite laugh at the flat joke.

"Speaking of real estate," he said, placing a folder on the table. "You're all set." He handed her a golden fountain pen with a small ink well.

"Wow, really old school." Lucy unscrewed the lid on the ink.

"I like signing contracts like this, it feels...I don't know. Big. Momentous." He said these little things with such passion, like every little detail mattered.

Lucy liked that.

Their gaze lingered a few seconds, before Lucy cracked open the folder. She dipped the pen in the well, oozy sticky liquid dripping out.

Blood instead of ink.

A drop plonked on the page as she hovered with the sharp tip above the dotted line. The blood snaked into a pulsating *"Lucy... did you miss me?"*Lucifera echoed in Lucy's mind. Sneering laughter, reverberating, fading in and out.

"Cold feet?" Matt asked, still smiling.

Lucy glanced up. Lucifera stood behind him, smirking wickedly. Holding a fountain pen of her own, she stabbed it into Matt's neck. Lucy gasped.

"Lucy?" he asked worriedly, "Are you all right?"

Lucy stammered, "I'm... just..."

His face turned pale fast. Meanwhile, Lucifera took her sweet time circling the table.

"Let me help you with that, bestie," the doppelgänger said playfully. She leaned in close and signed their name in

Matt's blood. "There you go..." She kissed Lucy on the cheek.

It took everything in Lucy to keep it cool.

"Ah, perfect."

Matt seemed to notice her shift in behaviour. Lucy handed the pen back and pushed the folder towards him slowly.

"I'll just give it a moment to dry..." he said. His bloodstain vanished, complexion natural once again. He left the file open on the side of the table; the ink well still uncapped.

Lucifera went back around behind him. "Look at you, Lucy, embracing yourself. Letting us all back in your life." She watched Matt with scrutiny, like she was thinking about what she might do next.

A faint, awkward smile from Lucy. She was seething inside. Lucifera had gone from best friend in childhood to the thorn in her neck that made her bleed every time she tried to look away. She wished she could hit her, pummel her face repeatedly under that stupid smirk fell off.

"Look, Lucy, if you're not a hundred percent about this, there aren't any other offers on the place right now," Matt said reassuringly. "There's no need to rush whatsoever." He slid the file back to her.

"Yeah, I'm...it's a big step. But you know what, it's best to just go on with it and jump into the cold water." She closed the file, handing it to Matt, forgetting all about the ink well. It spilled on the table and on her blouse and jeans. A splatter of black.

"Oh shit! Sorry..."

"No, I'm sorry," Matt said quickly, "me and my archaic tendencies. I'll get something for you to clean that up. Be right back."

Lucifera cackled. Nobody paid any more attention than a weird look at Lucy, a little shake of the head. Still wearing last night's pajamas, Lucifera took Matt's seat, lacing her fingers on the table.

"How I've longed for this day...and it's finally here. Sad though, that it takes death breathing down your neck to make you realise what you had all along was never a curse." She paused again. Now Lucy glared straight at Lucifera, not fiddling with any distractions.

"Yet you still won't acknowledge me," she went on. "Because you always cared more about what other people think. What will they say? Right? These strangers you'll never see again. Their opinion *matters*, doesn't it?"

Lucy bit her jaw, Lucifera's lip curled in a triumphant sneer. She knew how to push her buttons.

"Always trying to be normal. You realise you're living for everyone else. They don't care about you. But you want to be just like them, eh Lucy?"

Taking a deep breath through her nose, Lucy swore to herself she wouldn't let these games get to her. She leaned back in her chair., pretending to be nonchalant while she clenched her fists under the table.

"Answer me Lucy," Lucifera egged her on. "Say something Lucy. Lucy. Lucy. *Lucy. LUCY!*"A chorus of voices began overlapping each other. Louder. Messier. A billion crickets chirring insanely all at once.

Smirking, Lucy cocked her head to the side.

The voices ceased instantly.

"Look at you!" Lucifera beamed, dripping acid. "Beating me at my own game!" Hands up in defeat, she stood. "Impressive." She walked away with a sly smile.

Lucy was pleased with herself. Until a hand reached in from behind her, serving a plate onto the table. A dead crow, oozing blood onto the white dish. The head sprawled at an uncanny angle. Tiny black eyes staring blankly. Lucifera circled the table like a shark. Watching giddily.

Lucy couldn't take her eyes off the dead bird before her. "Stop it..." she murmured.

"Something wrong?" asked Lucifera.

"Stop," Lucy whispered indignantly. This was her mind, not Lucifera's—she was a *part* of her, not the other way around. Lucy was in control. No one else.

"Aren't you going to eat that?" Lucifera goaded.

The plate began vibrating, the crow's black feathers shaking violently, it snapped its head with a *crack* towards Lucy, cawing incessantly. She tried her breathing technique but the dish *stank*. She closed her eyes. Nothing helped. She could still hear that horrible scream, pungent smell getting overbearing.

"Shut up!" She swiped the dish onto the floor.

This was another high school moment. At least the other patrons at the restaurant weren't people Lucy would ever have to see again. Nonetheless, the way they stared at her uncomfortably, making her wish she was invisible. The waitress took two steps back, unsure how to proceed.

The shattered plate bore evidence of the salad that Lucy had ordered, now all over the floor. Lucifera was gone,

Lucy white with embarrassment. The bunch of strangers around her all waited for the crazy lady to make a move.

"I'm sorry," she said in a small voice. She dropped to the ground to start picking up the mess she made. Now the waitress hurried to her.

"It's okay," she said in her lovely Irish accent.

"No, I'm sorry. I'm very tired, I'm not being myself." Lucy almost cut her finger on a fragment of stained glass. "I'll clean this. Can you get me a broom?"

"Pathetic!" Lucifera's voice echoed.

"Please," the waitress persisted, "please no—*stop*. You'll hurt yourself." Lucy took a moment to compose herself.

"It's all right ma'am. I'll take care of it," the waitress said kindly, though tentative. Couldn't blame her. Lucy apologised once again.

"Here..." Counting bills, Lucy overpaid. "For the plate and the trouble." Dropping the cash on the table, she exited brusquely, keeping her head down. A few eyes just outside the restaurant followed her out the building.

Outside the clubhouse, Lucy stopped a passing golf cart. "Back to the hotel please."

"Everything all right, ma'am?" asked the driver, eyes pitch black, smile snaking across his lips. With a flash, his face melted to a frown—a glare—a ripple of indiscernible jagged lines. Back to a static expression with the beady black eyes.

Lucifera's laughter echoed. The others tried to shush her; it only got louder.

"Ma'am?" the cart driver pressed.

"To the castle. Please." Lucy made sure to avoid eye contact.

The driver nodded, seeming uneasy by Lucy's presence, a feeling she hadn't experienced in a while and didn't miss. All that angst she built up towards Lucifera over the years was rushing back. What else was there left to ruin? Why couldn't she just have one final act that was peaceful. She'd already wasted all her adult life in an illusion that she could have a normal life. She should have just accepted what she was from the start, dealt with them in her own way. Like any bully the best thing she could do was hit back harder. What exactly that meant, she wasn't sure, but she'd figure it out. If only for the sake of redeeming herself *from* herself.

Upon arriving, Lucy hurried toward the entrance, spotting a murder of crows circling the flags atop one of the turrets, cawing aggressively, taunting. She took a quick turn, breaching into the kempt grounds surrounding the citadel of a hotel. She found refuge behind a tree, leaning her back on it. Drawing in deep breaths. Sunlight danced through the leaves. It took her several moments to calm. The crows' ruckus vanished. Stealing a look back, not a single black bird fluttered about.

"*Bitch...*" she mumbled in an undertone. No one else was out here at the moment. Just Lucy. "Come on!"

No one showed.

"Come out you bitch!"

Laughing, Lucifera walked out from behind the large tree.

"You always do this!" Lucy pointed an accusing finger.

"It's not my problem you can't tell what's real! Besides, that was bloody hilarious," her doppelgänger retorted with a nonchalance that ignited Lucy further.

"Every time I'm happy, you have to glide in and ruin it!"

"Aww, play the victim Lucy, yes, it's all my fault." Lucifera rolled her eyes.

"You—" Lucy came up to her, face-to-face, "you and your bloody tricks!" Lucy poked her in the chest aggressively.

Lucifera's smile wilted.

"You did the exact same thing when we were sixteen," Lucy fumed. "When I started going out with Jeremy Goldberg you got so bloody jealous—"

"Jealous!? Of what? He was a freckled nerd!"

"*I* liked him."

"And you like this guy too, is that it?"

"*Like* him?" Lucy was utterly befuddled. "What the hell's wrong with you? I just signed a damn deed—opening a meadery was my dream since..."

"Our dream," Lucifera corrected.

"*My* dream!" Lucy snapped.

Lucifera glowered at her, but kept her mouth shut.

"That's your problem. It's all about you. Whenever something isn't done the way you deem fit. The way you find most comfortable in the most grotesquely selfish way, you start lashing out. Well, Lucifera, I'm at the bloody wheel!"

She gritted her teeth, "Don't call me Lucifera."

"You earned it with your stupid pranks." The next thing Lucy had on her mind was something she never said out loud before, and she wondered why, because it was so simple. "You're the reason I had to start taking clozapine."

"Mary's in charge of that fiasco."

"You still don't get it." An angry chuckle escaped Lucy's throat, she drew back a punch she knew would hurt, but what did she care, wasn't Lucifera just another part of her? "The others weren't the problem. You were the one who *never* let me rest. You're the reason we're fucking dying now."

Lucifera opened her mouth to retort. A shadow of regret clouded her stern glare.

"Just stay in the shadows," Lucy went on relentlessly. "Let me enjoy what's left."

Lucifera sniffed. Her lip quivered.

Circling the huge tree, Lucy walked away, back toward the castle's entrance. She could hear Lucifera's footsteps as she went in the other direction.

On the couch in her fancy room, she flicked through channels, landing on a music video where the singer, dressed in black, was burning in the sun. Sharp fangs protruding, his flesh cracked and peeled.

She opened a bag of muesli, munching on it in dry handfuls. Meanwhile, Lucinda was in the background, looking through a suitcase. American Luce's voice came from beside Lucy. She wasn't usually visible, but now her reflection showed from a round make-up mirror that had been lying on the couch. This one had a purple bob-cut, leaning her elbow on the couch's backrest.

"So, Lucy..." she said awkwardly, "that was crazy, huh? Lucifera's tricks..."

"Not talking about it," Lucy said curtly.

"Jeez Luce," Australian Lu sat beside her in the mirror. She had dark brown hair, long, straight. It didn't suit her. "You've got about the same amount of tact as a tractor."

Lucy rolled her eyes. She flicked the mirror away to reflect the ceiling instead.

"You need to get some real food in you," Lucinda said from behind.

"I like this song." Lucy turned up the volume. Tonight, she felt like wallowing and dry scooping muesli. She had the right to do that.

The others kept quiet. Lucinda plopped on the couch. Not at all a reflection, as Lucy felt the cushions move beside her. Unlike Luce and Lu, Lucinda was a main character in her brain.

They both sat in silence, watching two lovers on screen, in the night, the vampire playing violin for the woman, dancing.

"Look, even the misfit vampire found love."

"Love, eh?" Lucinda weighed her words. "I quite like this Matt character."

"It's not like that. He's just an estate agent. That's all."

"That's all?"

"Enough, Lucinda, please." Lucy yawned.

Lucinda glanced at something, no doubt a scowling Lucifera. Lucy kept her attention on the TV screen. "Not that it would have made a difference," she added.

Crows squawk. Tombstones. Fog. Soft snarling breaths. A towering, bulky silhouette carrying a woman...

- Chapter Five -
"No Turning Back"

A bold red *Sold* sign covered the previous one on the lawn of Castle Brewery. Sitting on the wide stairs, Lucy plugged in a pair of earphones and called her mother on video chat.

She answered immediately. Looking jaded, preoccupied, Mary was packing an *Open House* sign into the boot. Lucy could see she was getting into her parked car. A pang of guilt hit Lucy for how she made her mother worry. But she had to do this. It was her only chance of making a dream a reality. Trying treatments, which is what her Mum would vie for, would take too much time and energy and provide nothing but false hope. Lucy had already searched those avenues, scoured the internet. There was nothing to be found. Not even in the bottom of an ice-cream tub.

"Hi Mum." Lucy smiled. She kind of missed her.

"Lucinda Crowe!"

Maybe not that much...

"How dare you do that to me!?" Mary switched from indignant to relieved, then back to angry. "You know what went through my head when I saw that video message of yours? I don't even want to say it aloud."

"Oh no—Mum, I'd never do something like that..."

"Where have you been?"

"I just needed some time alone to...escape reality."

"Lucy, I..." Mary hesitated. Whatever she was bringing up was difficult for her to address. "I know we've had our differences, and I get that you're probably angry now."

"It's been an insane ride," Lucy interrupted. "No one could have predicted the outcome." She suddenly had the urge to reach out through the screen and hug her Mum. "Without your help, who knows, I'd probably be locked up in some place with pillows on the walls."

"You're scaring me with the way you're talking." Mary's eyes were red despite her firm expression. Resolute. "You need to come back home."

"I'm all right here." Lucy tried to sound as reassuring as possible.

"But you're all alone."

"I'm a big girl, Mum."

"God help me, Lucy, I will put up posters all over England until someone recognises you! You know I will."

"I'm not in England."

"In another country?"

"Relax Mum, I'm fine. Look..." She plastered on a wide smile. Her screen flickered, the little frame cracked, smoke whizzed out fissures. She paid no attention to it.

"And what about your meds? It's dangerous—"

"I'm taking my meds," she lied. A small fib at the end of time, big deal. Even so, it felt icky. "No visions whatsoever. Oh...low battery warning. Anyway, love you, Mum. I'll call again later. Send you some photos of the—" Lucy hung up. Battery still on 76%. She huffed, tired from the encounter, pocketing her cell. Opening the cutest mailbox, Lucy pulled out a set of keys and headed inside to begin her work.

Castle Brewery was quite the mess. Debris lay around, old casks, crates and bottles, boxes, and a ton of dust.

"No time to waste," Lucy said. "Maybe a little help?"

Lucinda walked out from an inner room. "You know I can't move things in your world, lass. Have you gone completely bonkers on me? Maybe when you get closer to death, I might be able to slip through the veil a little, when you're be closer to the other side."

"That is some heavy world building Lucinda."

"I don't make the rules."

"Tell me a story," Lucy said, judging the place, trying to figure out from where she should start. "Like those Dad used to read from his old fairytale collection."

"Ah-ha..." Lucinda cleared her throat; this was her element. "Now, you might be familiar with the name Bram Stoker. The legendary Irish author that introduced the world to Count Dracula."

"That's the stuff." Lucy found a large cardboard box, mostly empty. She cleared the place piece by piece as Lucinda went on with the tall tale. Some details Lucy felt like she was hearing for the first time. Must've forgotten those nuances—at least consciously.

"Stoker's story was inspired by vibrant Irish mythology. These folk tales, or 'historical accounts' as I call them..."

Lucy grinned, tossing cracked bottles and pieces of wood into the large carton.

"They go all the way from the foot-long Abhartach to the vengeful Dearg Due, leading the trail to Vlad the Impaler himself..."

It would take a while to get this place in shape, but at least Lucy had some company to pass the time.

That evening at the resort, Lucy entered with a plastic bag of groceries, tired but satisfied. The bored clerk at the front desk called out to her, "Madam! Excuse me, madam!"

Lucy looked over, stopped. A crack snaked on the wall behind him. Spread, widened, then reversed and vanished.

"Someone left this for you." He held out a plain brown package.

"For me?"

"You are Lucinda Crowe, yes?"

She closed the short distance between them. Hanging the grocery bag in the nook of her elbow, she tore open the package.

"You can wait," he protested, "open it in your room..." He sighed dejectedly, moving on to the customer behind Lucy, who had just walked in with a Chihuahua in her purse. "Oh, I'm sorry miss, but we don't let animals in here."

"It's my emotional support animal," the woman said as matter of fact.

"The only breed of emotional support we let in this resort is children. And those are already stretching it."

Lucy departed from the front desk. Her package was a blouse and pair of jeans with a note: *Sorry about the ink splash. Will switch to e-signing stuff after this note --Matt.*

She laughed to herself.

Lucinda trailed behind as she climbed the stairs. "He likes you," she said.

"Lucky, he didn't see the fiasco at the restaurant," Luce's voice came.

"Would have run from you like the plague if he knew how nuts you are," Lu echoed.

"That's mean," Luce said, taking offence herself.

"Although it is true," Lu defended.

"Do you think he's the one?" Luce asked, excited.

Lucy rolled her eyes. Beside her, Lucinda smirked. Lu was the one who spoke what they were thinking.

"The one?" she blurted, almost laughing.

"Yes, the one!" Luce persisted.

"No such thing as the one*"*.

"There's always the one—"

"Oh, shut up Luce, they've only hung out a couple of times!" Lu said, losing her patience.

Lucy huffed at her ridiculous inner dialogue, giving a shake of her head, smirking at Lucinda. She was used to this type of stuff. Everyone had thoughts with no filters, yet hearing them voiced was different. It used to make her feel foolish. Probably would have given her the same sense only a few weeks ago. However, at this point, she'd fully leaned into and accepted her 'minor' quirks. Looming death changed your priorities in an oddly liberating way.

"Hey Lucy," Lu chimed, *"I bet those pants don't fit you, fatty."* Her disembodied laughter echoed. It didn't bounce off the walls wickedly like Lucifera's, and Lu snorted a little sometimes.

"Guess I'll try 'em on." She reached the landing.

Lucinda stopped at the top of the stairs, looking back a few steps. Lucy caught a glimpse of Lucifera scowling. Did she want to be a part of the conversation? No, she was too bitter. Lucinda motioned for her to join them.

Lucy glanced sideways at the Celtic self, making sure not to meet her wicked doppelgänger's gaze. But Lucifera didn't overstay her welcome. Lucinda sighed wearily while Lucy headed for her room.

*

Mary let out a frustrated snarl. She checked her photos for the screenshot she grabbed just before Lucy disconnected the call. She zoomed in on the background. All she saw was a stone-faced wall and some cloudy sky.

"Damn it!" she hissed. Then her senses returned to her. "Oh, who am I kidding, I'm not bloody James Bond!"

Parking at a careless angle on two spots, Mary nicked another car as she opened her door. "Stupid car." It was too close. She awkwardly climbed over to the passenger side.

She pranced into the overly calm establishment. The perky lady in her twenties greeted Mary with a lively smile from the front desk.

"Morning ma'am, how can I help you today?"

Mary had no time for smiles and niceties. "I need your manager."

"Can I know why?" That annoying smile persisted. "I might be able to assist you. Our managers are a little busy at the moment."

"I need Lucinda Crowe's account details. Transaction history."

"So, your name is Lucinda Crowe, then..." She started typing on her keyboard.

"I'm Mary Crowe, her mother." Mary tapped her foot impatiently.

"I see," Perky nodded, "and how old is your daughter?"

"Thirty. Look lady—"

Perky clicked her tongue. "I'm sorry ma'am, but you'll need to bring your daughter in here with you. We can only disclose account information to her."

Mary leaned on the counter. "Get me your manager."

"Ma'am, even our manager is restricted by the same privacy laws that—"

"Listen to me Missy!" Mary was a kettle that just boiled. "My daughter is in danger, and *I* need to know where she is. So, get me your bloody manager *right now!*"

"I... Yes ma'am—Oh! there he is." She gestured to the branch manager who came out his office after hearing the rising voices out here.

"Hello?"

"I need my daughter's account history." Mary produced a few documents. "Here are her medical records and a letter from her psychiatrist." She smoothed those out on the counter.

The branch manager looked them over, then checked Mary's ID. "Hold on a moment." He made a quick call. "Hi yes, listen, I've got a situation here."

Mary waited anxiously for an answer. Perky was still smiling at her uncomfortably. Mary watched the manager closely as he nodded and bit his cheek.

"I see..." he said slowly.

This was the longest phone call Mary had ever experienced in her life, and she couldn't hear a thing that was happening at the other end.

She rushed out of the bank, worried as hell. Thumbing her phone angrily. Perky and the branch manager both watched her through the glass door as she hurried to the driver's side, haphazardly trying the door again, really dinging the car next to it.

Perky grimaced as the woman banged the door repeatedly until she squeezed in to the driver's seat and screeched off, already on her next call.

*

The brewery was starting to look a little better. The large, stainless-steel fermenters were still in the way, one of them fallen over in the middle of the room, as Lucy did anything she could around it. The cling and clang of dropping old glass bottles into a plastic bucket rang out. Two boxes full of junk near the door blocked it from opening fully when Matt's head popped in.

"Anybody home?"

Lucy straightened up, facing the door. "Matt. What are you doing here?"

"Stopped by the music store next door, thought I'd say hi."

"Welcome to my mess." She spread her arms.

Matt stepped in at the invitation. "It's looking good."

"Thanks for the new blouse, that was really kind of you."

Matt squatted down and helped Lucy pile glass into the bucket.

"You don't have to..."

Lucinda appeared at the scene. "Shut up lass!" she said fervently. "Go on, ask him something!"

Lucy continued picking scraps, filling a second small bucket. "So, what do you play?"

"Guitar."

"What kind of music do you like?"

"Folk, mostly."

"Finally, a straight answer from someone!"

"How do you mean?"

"You know those people that are like..." She switched to a deep voice. "Oh I like all music. I listen to anything."

Matt laughed. "You know what's worse? Those that say they don't *like* music."

"Those are dangerous. Turn and run."

"He should turn and run," Lucifera's voice taunted.

Lucy heated up, physically started sweating. She would have screamed at Lucifera to leave her alone. Yet, in truth, she knew Lucifera was right. What was she doing?

Matt emptied his bucket into one of the boxes before continuing. "So how about you—what's your kind of music?"

The spark had left the conversation. Just like that, one little comment ruined the mood. Out of pure defiance, Lucy decided she would fake having a good time if only to spite Lucifera, to spite *life*, for being such a bitch to her. So what if she wasn't staying for long? Even more reason for her to enjoy every last second to the fullest. If that meant some harmless flirting with the smitten estate agent, then so be it.

"I like mostly 80s and 90s stuff. And Elvis," Lucy said.

"Who doesn't like Elvis?" Matt said.

She nodded in agreement. Now that most of the glass was out the way, she started sweeping while Matt picked scraps of wood and debris from near the entrance.

"I don't mean to be too blunt, Matt, but I suppose I will. Do you usually buy jeans for your clients and help them clean rubble?"

"No," he said sheepishly.

"So," Lucy said, "Are you hitting on me?"

"Only in the most chivalrous sense."

Lucy swept the floor for a bit as Matt watched her for a reaction. "Full disclosure," she said finally, "I'm crazy."

"Believe me," Matt chuckled, "I can handle crazy. Grew up with six sisters."

"Six?" Lucy raised her eyebrows, stopped sweeping. "*Six?*"

Matt nodded.

"Are you Catholic or something?"

"Nope," he said. "My parents just like kids."

"Wow. Which one are you?"

"Of the sisters?"

Lucy rolled her eyes playfully.

Matt chortled. "Somewhere in the middle."

"Sandwich child. Poor you."

"You know, that's what they say, but I got whatever I wanted."

As they moved through the rubble, talking and working, Lucifera sat up in the rafters, watching them below, thoughts rippling behind her eyes. But she didn't interfere, not this time. Lucy was grateful for that.

The boot of Matt's car was open. He'd set up a gas burner with a pan on top. Now he was gently placing fillets on the hot oil with aggressive sizzles. Lucy sat by the pan on a three-legged camping chair.

"When you said you'll fix up lunch, I didn't think you meant this." Now she was having lunch with him? This was already going too far. She should stop it. She shouldn't lead someone on. This was wrong. It felt too right though. That defiance of hers popped back in with a vengeance. *Screw it,* Lucy thought, *I'm on a one way road out of here. I'll live it to the fullest.*

"I don't eat fast food, it's unhealthy."

"You're a strange man, Matt."

"I don't think I am." He sprinkled seasoning, then took a seat next to her on his own little folding chair.

"Those people do." Lucy pointed to a group of teens smoking and listening to Irish punk music off a tinny phone speaker. The bunch shared some laughs while glancing at them.

"What kind of fish are you making?" Lucy gestured to the simmering pan.

"Honeycomb salmon."

"I'm allergic to honey."

"Oh!" He slapped his forehead. "I should have asked. I'll go grab something else quickly." He stood, ready to go.

"I'm just kidding," she said and laughed. "I'm opening a meadery..." she chuckled.

"Okay," he sat back, the chair creaking a little. "Good. 'Cause I'm all out of moves."

"You could always sing," Lucy suggested, "got a guitar in your car?"

"I can't sing to save my life."

"See, now you have to sing for me, so I can be the judge of that."

"Maybe some other time."

"Ah." Lucy curled her lip. "So, there will be another time..."

"I should hope so." He watched her a little longer than usual, then moved his eyes back to the pan.

Lucy smiled. "So, this is your usual play to impress women? Music and cooking?"

"Don't take the magic out of it. Besides, honeycomb salmon is pretty much the only impressive dish I bothered learning to make."

"Why this dish?"

Matt got a reminiscent smile on his face that infected Lucy as he spoke. "When I was a kid, my father used to read me bedtime stories. In the books, the father cat made honeycomb salmon. I got hooked on that and begged my dad to make it for me. Rest is history."

"That's surprisingly sweet."

"Yeah, he seems a little too noice," Lu's Australian accent was far too suspicious.

"He's sweet!" Luce sounded starry-eyed.

"He's probably a psycho," Lu decided. *"Yup, definitely a psycho."*

Lucy swallowed, the voices giving her pause. She was alone in Ireland hanging out with someone she just met.

74

Should she be more cautious? A few moments passed in silence as the oil flickered in the pan. Why be afraid now? Now was the time to be fearless, she had nothing to lose! Why let the voices ruin something that might be good— no, it couldn't last, but that didn't matter. Lucy never had a bucket list, so she didn't have something to check off. Instead, she'd just let the wind blow her where it saw fit. Life had done its own thing anyway, so she may as well just give in a little. Though it was getting difficult to be in the present with all this circling in her brain. *Shut up!* she told herself.

"There's a nice restaurant here in Dublin," Matt said, "They have live music. I'm going to be performing there on Thursday night."

"Maybe I'll stop by."

Pleased, Matt poured some honey in the pan.

What am I doing? Lucy thought. She barely knew anything about this person she had randomly met. He was now cooking lunch for her and inviting her to his performance. Where was this going? She was sure it wouldn't get too far. None of her relationships had, if any of them could have been considered relationships until this point. For now, she was just going on a date, something she hadn't done in forever.

"Is this heather honey?" Lucy swallowed a savoury bite. They were halfway through the meal, plates on their knees.

"I actually don't know." He checked the jar. "Wow, you know your honey."

"I make mead, remember," she said.

"So, you're a mead maker, and I'm a Viking, right?"

"Your hair, not mine." Lucy shifted in her seat to face him, mischievous. "Okay, let's make a deal."

"What deal?"

"I'll make a small batch—so that you can reconnect to your true Viking heritage—and you'll sing in front of me."

"Wow, Lucy, moving so fast." He shook his head, giving it some deep thought. "Aye."

Lucy put out a hand. Matt shook. "It's a deal," she said.

He handed her the jar of heather honey.

Clothes on the bed, Lucy was trying to pick which outfit to go with. Lucinda was with her. Over the last few weeks, it felt like Lucy had reconnected with a long-lost friend. It was good to have her back. Somehow, this time when she'd stood up to Lucifera, it actually helped. Perhaps the intensity of the situation made a difference. Whatever it was, Lucy found herself regretting the fact that she'd missed out on this all these years. *No regrets,* she told herself. No time to waste on that.

"Try this one," she told Lucinda.

The Celtic witch pranced along the room as if she was on a catwalk, red curls bobbing. Lucinda snapped her fingers and her outfit morphed into the blue dress Lucy had suggested. She gave it a twirl, batting her eyelashes.

Lucy laughed. At the back of the room, Lucifera stood with her arms folded. Lucy ignored her.

"My hair colour's not the same," Lucinda said, "you could always ask—"

"No," said Lucy, curtly. She deflated a little, picked out something else she liked. Jeans and a loose, white buttoned shirt.

"Hold your horses, it's not a wedding," Lucifera murmured. "Don't get too fancy."

"Are you just coming to sulk?" Lucy snapped. She turned to Lucinda. "Can't you lock her in a cage or something, so I won't have to see that annoying face?"

Lu's Australian voice came in a mutter. *"Better cover the mirrors in the house too..."*

Lucy gave a contemptuous look to the air around her, scoffing at the unseen Lu. She turned her attention back to Lucifera—Lucy's spitting image but in pajamas. The same ones that Lucy had gotten as a gift from her dad when she was six. She remembered them until now. Had them in the same treasure box she kept at home with her old things. But Lucifera's pair had grown with her.

"Go away, Lucifera," she said.

"I told you not to call me that."

"I've had enough of this! I'm..." Lucy bit her jaw, "...dying."

"*We're* dying," Lucifera interjected.

"Yes," Lucy said, "*we're* dying. All of us! And all you're doing is trying to screw up what's left."

"So, when are you going to tell Matt that there's not much time for the two of you?"

"Don't you dare play one of your stupid tricks on me tonight."

Lucifera raised her hands. "Couldn't if I wanted. I'm not at the wheel, am I?"

"No, you're not."

"Yeah," Lu chimed, *"she's been meditating."*

"Lu, shut up!" Lucy yelled, agitated by her aloofness, "I'm not stuffing around."

"Relax, babe," Lucifera moaned, "I'm not interfering. I actually want to see how this all goes to shit in a few weeks."

She snapped her fingers, using Lucinda's trick, and was suddenly wearing a maroon dress. She gave Lucy a 'holier than thou' smirk and walked out of the room.

Lucy eyed her contemptuously. "Bitch..."

"I know," Luce spoke for the first time that night, *"that dress looks* killer *on you."*

"I told you to pack it, but you never listen," Lu added.

Lucy faced the bed, picking out her jacket that looked plainer than plain.

People buzzed about outside a pub named Folklord Tavern. Lucy made her way in. She generally didn't like these sorts of places, but thankfully no one was smoking in here and it had an appealing aesthetic. Far more than she'd expected initially.

The place was well-lit, not bright. No one on the small stage at present. Music played from speakers. The other two were with Lucy.

"Oh, look at that!" Lu piped up.

Lucy cocked her head in the direction of the voice. A bulky chandelier made of guitars, cymbals and trumpets hung up there.

"Wow, that is badass," Luce said.

Lucifera kept to the back. Lucinda hung there for a moment.

"Nice place, eh?" she said.

"I thought you hate these places," said Lucifera.

Lucinda shrugged. "I do it for her."

They both looked at Lucy, who glanced back at them. She locked eyes with Lucifera. Tension taut as a cello string.

"You two have got to work out your shite," Lucinda said.

Lucifera didn't stop staring at Lucy with acidity. "Let's just enjoy the music."

"Oh, I plan on it." Lucinda produced a pair of earplugs to block out the noise.

Lucy grabbed a stool at the bar. As soon as she sat, a goatee guy dressed in hip clothing brushed past her. He gave Lucy a warm, friendly smile. Too friendly. A little drunk. Lucy grinned awkwardly, hoping he'd piss off.

"*Argcodlaíonntúar do bholg? Armhísteleatlígeandomsa?*" he asked, reeking of whiskey.

Lucinda gasped and whispered in Lucy's ear, which made Lucy scoff as well at how downright rude that was. Gross.

"*Dóagusbascadh ort!*" Lucy replied haughtily.

The goatee guy was at a loss for words. "Oops..." The man walked away with a hiccup; someone shoved him out their way as they walked past.

The bartender asked from the side, "Can I get you anything, miss?"

"Guinness draught, thanks."

"I'll have one of those, too." Matt emerged from the crowd. The bartender didn't seem to hear him though, and only got one beer.

"Another one, please," Lucy told him.

He nodded happily, got another bottle and moved on to the next customer.

"This is a nice place. I love that chandelier." Lucy said, looking up again, she saw bats hanging upside down in various spots on the ceiling.

Matt wasn't very talkative, and looked really nervous.

"When are you on?" she asked.

"Any minute now." He had a few gulps.

"Is this your first time performing in front of such a big crowd?"

"Done this a hundred times actually."

"Then why so nervous?"

"In my head I've got more on the line."

"Oh..." She grinned.

"Aye, there's a talent agent in the crowd that I'm hoping to impress."

"Oh."

Matt took in her reaction. "I'm just messing with you. Getting you back for telling me you were allergic to fish!"

Lucy kicked him playfully in the shin.

"All right, wish me luck." Leaving his unfinished beer on the countertop, Matt went for the stage. A band waited up there. He muttered something to the drummer, bassist and keyboard player. They nodded. One of them gave him a thumbs up.

Ready for the show, Lucy sat up straighter. Her spot at the corner of the bar gave a good view of the stage. Everyone else was busy with their meals and conversations. Not much attention was given to the live performance when the drummer counted Matt in.

Crisp, clean Celtic music.

A jig-worthy tune climbing up and down rhythmically. Some people glanced up from their tables.

Lucy was loving it. Even Lucinda took out her ear plugs.

Readying his foot over a pedal, Matt nodded to the drummer, who picked up tempo. And...

Distortion.

It was still Celtic music, but significantly heavier. Lively folk rock at high speeds with higher notes. Matt was in the zone.

Lucy laughed to herself. The bartender leaned next to her again, watching the stage.

"He's great, isn't he?" Lucy asked.

"Meh..."

Lucinda plugged up her ears again, shaking her head at the sacrilege. Lucifera watched Matt up on stage, still wearing that maroon dress, arms folded, her face made of stone, tapping her foot despite her moodiness. Lucy's lip curled. In one of the glasses was Luce's reflection in the crowd, her purple hair bouncing as she bobbed her head wildly, dancing to the music.

Turning her attention back to the stage, Lucy saw no one else in the room. Literally just Matt and her. The stage was empty, too, and all she could hear was the guitar. Lights played games with lively colours.

Still shredding, Matt stole a look at Lucy across the floor.

A picture-perfect moment.

"That is insane! I can't believe you got away with it!" Matt laughed. The plates on their table were mostly empty. Lucy took the last bite of a chocolate cake.

"Although catching you head-banging in the crowd would have been a sight to see."

"Yeah, imagine that. With purple hair and all."

Matt laughed again.

"Wait..."

Did he say 'Lucy—Lucy' or 'Lucy Goosey?' "Did you just call me Lucy Goosey?" She was sure she heard it wrong.

"No—why, is that your preferred nickname?" he asked, frowning, "'cause I don't think I can bring myself to say it."

"No, please don't. My father used to call me that when I was little."

"What's he like?" Matt listened for an answer like she was the only person in the world worth listening to.

"He's...you know, he's wonderful. Taught me how to ride a bike, took me on camping trips, he really got me into folklore. He was an historian." When she spoke about her father, Lucy got lost in the story, a mosaic of love and ache. Longing.

Matt didn't just listen; he drank her in.

"He was the best dad ever," Lucy said. "Like an actual fairy tale. And like an actual fairy tale, he got a heart attack when I was seven."

"I'm so sorry."

"Then another one when I was eight."

"Oh."

"And that was it. Still miss him...he's one of the reasons I came to Ireland."

"How so?"

"Always told me stories about how magical this place is."

"It is magical," Matt said, staring into her eyes.

"What about your parents?" she asked, moving the spotlight off herself eagerly.

"Dad's a musician."

"Did he teach you guitar?"

"Nah," Matt said, "his instrument is bagpipes."

"How very Celtic."

"He tried to teach me. But I wasn't interested in McCall." Matt shrugged. "So instead, I kept trying to play metal on bagpipes."

"Oh God, that's got to be a new form of torture."

"My oldest sister saved us all the misery and bought me an electric guitar for my birthday."

"Your dad was all right with that?"

"That's when I got kicked out the house," he joked. "So, I was wondering, Lucy, you're an accountant."

She could smell his cologne, like a fresh suit.

"But you want to open a meadery," he went on, touching on something she was afraid would come to light too soon. It was becoming increasingly clear that this was no longer just a harmless date. "Why now?" Matt asked.

"I don't know." She'd been prepared for something like this. But hiding the truth from him felt so wrong when he'd been so genuine to her up until now. Lucy could never know for sure. Yet she wouldn't just spill the beans. A little more time. This may well still go nowhere. She wasn't about to trusting her emotional capacity. So, she kept all that at bay for the time being.

"Just an impulse I guess," she said. "Wanted something different. I've always been very *methodical* about life. Had it all planned out. I needed something to get me out of the rut."

He watched her silently. Thoughts shaping in his mind from the looks of it. "You're something else, aren't you?"

"What makes you say that?"

"That night at the hotel last week—I felt like there was magic." He waved dismissively. "I know, it sounds stupid but, what can I say? It was strange."

"So, you believe in magic?"

"Of course."

Lucy was puzzled by how serious he was. "For real?"

"Yeah, how else would you explain love?"

Whoa. Cat got Lucy's tongue. She had no response to this. Matt laughed in his booming voice.

"I didn't mean it like that!" he gestured. "I haven't known you for long enough, Lucy. I'm just saying, the whole idea of it, it's not logical. Evolution, survival of the fittest. None of that explains it. Not enough for me." He looked off to the side, thoughtful, maybe a little distracted, definitely a little red on the cheeks. "Anyway, I'm rambling and embarrassing myself...it's hot in here."

Smiling, Lucy eased up again.

"Sometimes I don't realise how things sound before I blurt them out." Matt waited for a moment. "Could you please say something?"

"No, no...you're doing great. I'm enjoying this thoroughly, please proceed," she teased.

Matt beamed at her. "You've got, like, five different sides to you."

Lucy snickered. If only he knew.

"And I want to get to know all of them," Matt said plainly. Honestly.

Lucy hadn't seen them there until now, but off to the side of their table, Lucinda raised her eyebrows at Lucifera. Something changed in her demeanour. Lucifera wasn't glaring as usual, which made her seem a tiny bit less hostile, even if only a smidge less.

- The Crowe -

The crow watches, intrigued by these two, mostly the woman though. Since she arrived in this country, it's been interested in her, remembering her face from the airport. That's how it found her at the huge stone nest that she lived in. She is interesting. Why? The crow can't tell; it just knows that she is. That is enough, because there's never any need to give an explanation to anyone. It is a crow. That is the beauty.

He calls her Lucy, and she calls him Matt.

Interesting.

Honey dribbles into a glass carboy in copious amounts.

Dressed for the night, Lucy applies lipstick in front of the mirror.

Matt and Lucy walk through the aisles of a shopping centre. He picks up a jar of honey, to which she shakes her head. The crow recognises that motion. It means no.

Using Matt's chairs and the cooler box as a table, Lucy and he play a game with a chequered board and tiny, strange animal figures, none of them are particularly shiny. But the people are eating sandwiches.

At her instruction, Lucy and Matt are now making something with the honey. They call it "mead." The equipment isn't extensive. A glass bottle—shiny—a bucket filled with foaming stuff, powder that smells almost like beer, honey. That's it. Matt licks honey off his fingers, hands Lucy a strange curvy pipe. She pours sanitizer all over it, scrubbing. Matt dips his hands in the foaming bucket. The bubbles glitter beautifully in the sunlight.

The door to the bathroom in the castle is open, visible through the windowsill from outside. Lucy and Lucinda stand in front of the mirror, each doing her own thing. Lucy clasps her lips down on a folded tissue, then checks her teeth to make sure there's no lipstick on them. Lucinda keeps poofing in and out of different outfits with waves of her hand.

A shipment of brewing supplies arrives at Lucy's meadery. Inside, the place looks a whole lot better. A lot of work's been put into it. It's starting to get the semblance of an establishment.

Lucy and Matt stand at the till, and she's gaping at the teller while Matt loads honey in the trolley.

In the middle of this game, Lucy reaches for a pointy artifact. Lucinda catches her hand mid-motion. Points to an ugly horse. Changing tactics, Lucy gets the upper hand. Matt thinks harder. Lucy takes a bite, relaxed.

Vigorously shaking the honeyed water in the glass carboy, Matt turns the motion into an awkward dance with the way he steps, putting a little rhythm into it, looking ridiculous, making Lucy laugh.

Then he sings...as promised. And it's horrid.

Perched on a windowsill, the crow watches them curiously.

At night, Lucy walks out Cleland Castle Retreat, alone. Lucifera's behind her as the door closes, thoughtful.

At the shopping centre, the teller is someone familiar to Lucy—the hairy, ripped, shirtless, ram-headed Gravedigger—picking up one of six jars of honey, the beast snorts, then beeps it through.

At their artifact game, Lucy wins. Matt has no idea how she pulled it off. He drops his sandwich by mistake; Lucy gives him half of hers. The crow focuses on the fallen piece of food. There's a slice of meat in there.

Once Lucy and Matt leave the brewery, the crow on the sill eyes a bee buzzing about—it pecks at it, gobbles it down.

Wearing the same outfit she just inspected in the bathroom of her hotel room, Lucy meets Matt, and they head out.

At the brewery, electric pumps, vats of honey, siphons— new words, new fermentation equipment. It's all in the middle of the clean, freshly painted meadery. The crow can't remember when it learnt these words. Maybe it just always knew them.

Leaving the shopping centre, Lucy looks over her shoulder. The beastly gravedigger helps the next customer, not even throwing a glance in her direction...

Sometimes Lucy had weird dreams. As if her mind wasn't strange enough when she was awake, it still enjoyed making a sizzle reel summarising the last few weeks with Matt in a mess of confusion and hazy, blurring timelines. She vaguely remembered a crow eating a bee—or did *she* eat the bee? It was all slipping away so fast, as dreams often did.

- Chapter Six -
"It's Magic"

Lucy's life was generally free of regrets, except for the big one. It had always gnawed at her from the dark depths of the subconscious, where she'd failed to bury it. Doing everything meticulously left no room for impulsivity, and life was, by nature, sporadic. That she'd learnt more than anything in recent weeks. And if she were afraid that she had wasted time hiding in routine, not really living, then these last few weeks washed everything away.

Finding love was something that had always allured her, and something she always feared. However, as she sat on a bench in a park with Matt, watching other people mill about, some other couples, Lucy found herself no longer wondering. Of course she wasn't in love with the man. Not yet. Everything was still fresh and glittery, and she knew it couldn't last. The banshee had keened, as Lucinda had said. But it was so easy with Matt. So simple. When it would get to the 'not easy' part, she would find out if this was something real or not. And by then, it would be too late.

Lucy swore to herself she'd tell Matt the truth. All of it. These 'simple dates' were more than that now. It wasn't right to lead someone on. Hurt them. This was probably what drugs felt like to people who were addicted. *You know you have to stop, but you don't want to quit the feeling 'cause it's way too damn good,* she thought.

"You said you believed in magic," Lucy said.

"Aye."

"I got a taste of it these last few weeks." She leaned on Matt's shoulder and he wrapped his arm around her, on cloud nine. Lucy was a knot of unspoken emotions. Matt's affection felt so good, so right, that it cut her like a knife.

She didn't speak after that, lost in the twilit sky. Matt was all right with the quiet, they didn't need to fill the silence. Lucy tensed up a little when Lucifera took a seat beside them.

Her doppelgänger smelt the wild evening air, glanced sideways at her tortured counterpart. "And now the realisation sets in," she said, riddled with pity, "when are you going to do it?"

Lucy did not answer, but the flicker of her eyes, gazing forward at nothing, could have said everything.

"Ever wondered why Matt is so sweet, so *perfect?*" she scoffed, mumbling, "I wonder if he's even really here."

Cheap shot. Lucy thought.

Lucifera looked to Matt. "She's dying. This won't last long. Are you all right with that?" Shaking her head with disappointment, Lucifera stood. "Axe is coming down, Lucy." She left, but her voice echoed, disembodied, with one last, *"Tick... Tock..."*

The breath caught in Lucy's throat until she actively eased up. She was going to tell Matt—even if not right now. Still, it's all she could think about lately. One way or the other, the truth was coming out.

Lucy and Matt walked abreast in the hallway of Cleland Castle Retreat. Some of the black tiles blinked when they stepped on them. She unlocked the door.

"You've been awfully quiet all night," Matt said.

"Lots going on in here." Lucy tapped her skull.

"Good or bad?"

She gave him a strained smile. Her phone rang, an upbeat Celtic lute tune. A call from *Mum*. Lucy disconnected it, not before seeing the six unread messages. She set her phone to silent.

"Matt..."

His face fell, the vestiges of a smile looking like a grimace.

"There's something I need to—"

He kissed her.

She was surprised, but didn't stop him.

When they pulled apart, Lucinda was smiling from ear to ear, watching the two silently.

"Okay..." Lucy blubbered.

"I just...didn't want to be on my death bed and think what if," Matt said, but seemed to regret his choice of words immediately.

Lucy watched him for a long bloody time, her mouth still slightly agape. Mind racing.

"Well don't just stand there." Lucinda poked her in the ribs. "Say something, you oaf!"

"I... I'm..." Lucy's chest heaved, "I'm crazy."

Matt snickered. He didn't get it, seemingly confused about whether this was code for something good or bad.

"Literally," Lucy barreled on, heart against all the stops in her head, like a rhino rampaging through a fine restaurant. "I have schizophrenia."

And she waited.

Matt didn't seem to know how to digest this point-blank. His eyes flitted hither and thither. He gave a little bit of a slow nod. When this started, Lucy didn't think she could be terrified of anything anymore. And yet, the thing she feared most was not a tombstone, it was the sight of Matt running back down the stairs. She'd felt it in the past, a very long time ago. Couldn't even remember that other guy's name. But Matt's name—that she'd never forget. Never. It wasn't even a choice at this point. Unlike the time before, this silence was hell. Lucy couldn't read him.

Matt took a step back, pointed at her with furrowed brows, mouth twisting. it looked like he had a thought that almost formed into a word but came out as a sigh. Lucy wished she could hide under a hoodie or bury her head in a mound of sand.

"Do you change?" he finally asked.

"I—no," Lucy said, "I don't have dissociative identity disorder. It's different. It's more external to me and..."

"Oh. So you see things? That aren't there?" Matt stood rooted.

At least he didn't take another step back.

"Well, the voices say it's magic," Lucy rambled, "that I'm a refraction of sorts and—"

"Why are you telling me this?" Matt finished. "Why now? Suddenly."

"Because I'm..." Lucy paused.

Lucinda would be on the edge of her seat if she had one.

"How do you know I'm real?" Matt asked. "How are you not more freaked out?" Lucy said.

"I am." Matt shrugged. "I think."

Lucy came closer to him and he still didn't move, which gave her the smallest reprieve. "Then why are you still standing here."

Matt regarded her in that same way he had back at the table of the Folklord Tavern.

"Why are you still here, Matt?"

"Because I can't just walk away," that confused portrait of his face—the shock—turned to clear realisation. "I don't know, maybe it's magic or something."

"Wow, making jokes already. I don't know if that's a good sign—"

"No Lucy." He half smiled for a brief second. "I mean, I think it's *magic*."

Lucy stared at him. "As in..." *love?* She didn't say that out loud. But that's what he'd called magic before. Is that what he meant? She was too stunned to carry on talking. She didn't even allow herself to think that way. Not really. None of this was serious. This was never going to get far enough. Lucy wasn't planning on staying long enough for this to happen.

"This wasn't supposed to happen," she said.

"What was supposed to happen?" Matt asked.

Both of them stood there on a precipice.

"I don't care." Lucy also didn't care to think what might happen next. She stopped thinking, and let herself feel. Only feel. It wasn't lust. It wasn't yearning. It wasn't meant to be. It was freedom. Maybe Matt was right. Maybe it was just magic. She took the leap.

Lucy coiled her arms around Matt's neck. Kissed him. Pulled back. They got lost in each other's eyes. He moved in close. Kissing her again. Tangled in each other. Like they've been holding back for ages. Yearning.

Lucy wrapped her legs around his waist, never pulling apart. Matt lifted her up. Stumbling into Lucy's room, he fell with his back on the mattress with a soft thud. Lucy couldn't even remember how or when they'd unlocked the door. Were there keys to that door?

Her hair hid his face in a blonde veil. The two of them moving in sync, like choreography. Music. The only moments Lucy and Matt moved away from each other were the brief snippets to remove items of clothing intermittently. Wind washed into the room, breathing life into the silky white curtains.

Crows squawking. Tombstones. Fog. Soft snarling breaths. A towering, bulky silhouette carrying a woman...

Lucy rested her head on Matt's chest. She was wide awake while he slept. Looking up at his face, she smiled. Matt shifted, pulling Lucy a little closer. That blissful smile stayed on Lucy's face as she closed her eyes.

Then she peeked at the window, thinking she'd glimpsed Lucifera sitting there. The curtain billowed. She snuggled up closer to Matt. But damn it, now she couldn't sleep, because her mind was working again.

- Chapter Seven -
"A Stake to the Heart"

Matt's car trailed between breathtaking hues, the vehicle getting lost in the leaves and sunset. Between the trees Lucy caught glimpses of a castle. And then the thicket thickened, blocking all view. A winding maze of vibrant greens and fiery red climbed up a small hill.

"Beautiful, isn't it?" she asked.

"Beyond incredible," Matt said, "but don't change the subject."

"Come on, you can't be serious."

"Why not? There's so much we don't know about the world. Look, why did you choose Ireland, of all places?"

"It's always been my dream to open a meadery here."

"Ok. Then why now?"

Lucy didn't respond. She'd told him one part of the truth, but she never thought they would have survived past that. Now it was even harder to spill the rest.

"Who suggested Ireland to you?" Matt pressed, grinning.

"So, what's your point?" asked Lucy.

"The Celtic witch. Lucille?"

"Lucinda..."

"She's got to know something—assuming she's actually a witch—and what are the odds that we cross paths?"

"You're telling me that magic brought us together?" She could not believe what she was hearing.

"Aye. I don't believe in coincidence."

Lucy beamed at him. "Matt Cunningham, I think you might be weirder than me."

"Maybe so, but that means I'm right."

"Because what are the odds?"

Smash!

A black bird in the windscreen.

Matt lost control of the vehicle for just a fraction of a second. Tyres screamed to a stop and a bloody crack appeared on the windscreen.

"Bloody hell..."

"It was a raven. I think." He and Lucy hurried out.

She bent down a few paces behind the car. "Argh hell..." A messy clump of black feathers lay limp on the tarmac, ruffling in the breeze.

"Poor raven," Matt said.

"It's a crow." Lucy felt an odd prickle at the back of her neck, trailing icy cold down her spine, raising the hairs on her skin. This time, the crow was not in her head.

"There's a difference?"

No other cars drove past.

"I'll move it out the street," Matt said, rummaging around in the shrubbery off the shoulder of the road, he found a stick.

A drop of blood fell from Lucy's nostril. She didn't notice when she hit her nose, probably when Matt stopped the car suddenly. She wiped it with the sleeve of her long cardigan. Something about the crow was hypnotizing. She could feel something coming on. Something looming. Something different.

With jerky, uneven motions, the dead bird twisted its contorted head, spoke to Lucy in a scratchy, deep voice. *"Dearg Due is coming."*

"Let's get you off here," Matt said and pushed the crow to the descending shoulder, into the thicket. As he dragged the creature across the road, its head stayed zeroed in on Lucy like a magnet pull. And it didn't shut up.

"Dearg Due. Dearg Due..."

Once they were back on the road, Lucy was rattled, not present.

"You all right there?"

It took her time. "Fine. I've just been seeing a lot of crows lately."

"Does it mean something?"

"Huh? No—not that I know."

"Well, it's a hell of an introduction to some rickety old castle."

She wore a smile. Didn't feel it. "Most definitely is."

Matt said nothing. Instead, he reached over and held her hand in his as he drove on. Lucy closed her fingers, staring out the window, her biggest secret still weighing on her. She didn't want to think about that now. She squeezed his hand a bit. Pushing her looming thoughts down just a little further, the engine sputtered like a hungry beast, moving off toward the castle up the hill.

Lucy's long, red cardigan flapped lazily in the breeze. She and Matt went up the path toward the ruins. A skeleton of a castle sprouted out the earth. Vines and moss had taken over. The bulk of the thing was caved in, but the way it guarded the land it was on, Dunhill Castle was imposing.

"Wow..." Matt looked up at the relic in awe. "I've never been here. Your Dad told you of this place?"

Lucy nodded. "His ancestors lived here at some point."

"Royalty?"

"Farmers. Come on." The two of them circled the building to where a portion of the wall bulged out, aging bricks shaped oddly like a head. The stone ground, head-like vestige turning very slightly to face Lucy, its features an enigma of moss and creepers. She paused for a second. It was like finding shapes in clouds, the face gone just as it had come.

"This place must have a million stories to tell," Matt said, entranced by the old stones.

"Yeah," Lucy found herself unable to enjoy this as she wished she could have. She felt she was standing on the precipice of something. The universe mocked her, throwing a crow into their windscreen. Telling herself she was at the wheel didn't feel as reassuring as it once did. She led the way into the structure.

Sunlight spilled through the top, where the ceiling used to be. The outer walls were mostly gone, vines everywhere. Nature had made this manmade thing its own.

"Up here," Matt said.

An old staircase, totally exposed to the outside air, provided enough room for them to climb single file to the top of the tower. No more than two storeys high. The floor was also the ceiling, because there was nothing left of the castle above this point.

"Look at that..." Lucy drew in the fresh air. "Life at its fullest."

The landscape was a canvas of green shades, so many that no other colour was needed. For a split-second Lucy forgot herself. It was overwhelming. Primal. The way the light played on her face, the wind. Tears welled up in her eyes, she laughed happily. Matt, too, totally mesmerised by her. Right here, right now, it was a full lifetime in a few heartbeats, and it meant everything. Lucy wiped her eyes. Beamed at Matt. They shared a kiss up there on that tower. Matt then pulled a vial out of his pocket, sealed it with a cork. Lucy couldn't help laughing at his theatrics.

"Now I can hold onto this moment forever."

"You could just take a photo," she joked.

He just kissed her again. "Any fairy tales you know about this castle?"

"Well..." Leading the way back down the stairs, Lucy walked ahead into what was left of the tower's room. She peered out the small windows as she spoke. "We're in Waterford, so there is the Dearg Due." Something ground again. Stone on stone.

A beat.

Not a sound.

When she turned, the room was closed off. A wall where there was none. A closed door, too. Matt had vanished from sight. It gradually got darker. She took a deep breath. Tried to control the vision, yet this time it felt more real than real. She reached for the door handle of the arched exit in front of her. It *clicked* before she touched it.

With a whine, the thing opened up letting in a dark figure, obscured by the intensifying shadows. His face was cast in shadow, save for the red eyes, the angle of his chin.

Lucy composed herself. *It's not real.*

The enigma clicked his tongue. "This old dump. Wish you'd have come to my home in Transylvania. Convinced Bram Stoker to set his story there after I spoke to him..."

"You've got to be kidding me," Lucy scoffed. "A new one?"

"*Dun-dun-duuun,*" he declared dramatically.

Lucy couldn't see any distinctive features. It was far too dark. The only source of light shimmered from the creature's red irises, faint like a dying wick.

"Not now," she stated adamantly.

"If I am not for me, who is? And when I am for myself, what am I? And if not now, then *when*?"

Lucy got antsy. "I knew this was coming," angry that she was seeing this shit, she pushed past him.

The dark figure grabbed her arms, spun her around roughly. She'd felt them before, little snippets of a hand brushing hers.

"Is that *real* enough for you?" His pupils morphed into slits.

Lucy stared at him in terror. Looked down at the clasping hands. Mist swirled around them serenely.

The demonic eyes slunk back to human form. "I just want to talk, Lucinda." He let go, towering above her. "You're fleeing death."

No response from Lucy.

"I'm quite the expert in that department."

"And who might you be?"

"The name's Vlad."

"As in Vlad the Impaler?"

"The one and only."

"In Ireland?" She thought about how this might appear to Matt from the outside, seeing her talk to thin air. Not a good look despite him knowing about her condition. There's knowing and there's seeing.

"I've lived all around Lucy. Where do you think Bram Stoker got his inspiration? Instead of looking for plot holes," Vlad hissed arrogantly, "maybe you should be thinking about how you're going to get yourself out of this one."

"Enlighten me," she kept trying to use responses that didn't give away the fact that she was dying. She would tell Matt. She swore she would. Just not like this.

"You never feared death before."

Lucy resumed her pace. So what if this vision embodied Vlad the Impaler? She should have left that damn *Dracula* novel back in England instead of giving her mind fresh material to use against her.

"Until now..." he added softly. "Yes, now the great fearless Lucinda fears death."

She stopped, reaching a wall.

"That is a symptom of love, my dear." Cutting the distance between them once again, Vlad put his hands on Lucy's shoulders. "Do you know why I'm helping you, Lucinda? My blood runs in your veins. I lost my love, tried to bring her back, but she was never the same. I hope you never have the pleasure of meeting her. Besides, I'm really a sucker for a good love story..."

"How touching."

He sank his teeth into her neck, eyes turning to slits again. Lucy grunted, gasped. And then Vlad stood there in front of her. As if he'd glitched, and was never touching her in the first place.

She wasn't perturbed. She knew he wasn't real. She still rubbed her neck though, it burned from the inside venom.

"Shit," Lucy mumbled. If in addition to seeing and hearing, she was starting to *feel* things that weren't there, she was spiraling way too far way too fast.

These visions were beginning to get out of hand fast. Maybe her medication was what brought death to her doorstep, but she was beginning to realise that it might have been the one thing that gave her the opportunity to have normalcy up until that point she chucked it out the window.

"The banshee has keened," Vlad repeated Lucinda's words.

"I don't need to hear this," she said, feeling like her blood was buzzing in her veins. It was getting darker. the air was dank too.

"The sand runs thin, Lucy."

"Shut up—"

"Time isn't on your side." He came closer to her, too close. "And you're standing here, *wasting* the little bit you have left pretending—"

"I don't need you to remind me the sand's running thin!" Lucy hissed at him through gritted teeth. "Now piss off!" She shoved him, hard. And her hands met a solid mass. She took a step back—truly horrified by her visions for the first time.

Vlad's teeth showed in a smile. He won this little game she didn't know she was playing. And then Lucy realised her mistake. She thought perhaps Matt would never have heard the low whisper, but she could smell his cologne now. Unfortunately, as was the way with words, once they were out, they didn't belong to you anymore.

Light faded back in, and the illusion misted away. Matt stood in Vlad's place. Matt, who'd been standing there the entire time. Matt, whose eyes searched—no, *begged* Lucy's face for some sort of explanation.

"What do you mean, Lucy?"

She tried to say something. Words failed her the first few times. "Nothing," she tried to brush it off. "I'm sorry you had to see that, Matt."

"I'm not," his eyes were red with fury. A betrayal Lucy could tell he would never forgive, And yet, there was something vulnerable about him, even in this moment. "I tried talking to you. You didn't see me?"

With the state he was in, Lucy wished he would take a step back this time.

She simply shook her head.

"The things you said. What did you mean by the sand running thin?" Matt searched her face.

"It means..." She hated this, but it was bound to happen. Lucifera stood behind Matt, shaking her head 'I told you so'. Lucy hated her for that right now.

"It doesn't mean anything Matt."

"Don't lie to me," he said. "Not now!"

"Why not!?" Lucy heated up. He still didn't back off, she too stood her ground. "So what if I lie? It doesn't make a difference. It *can't*. Nothing can change my future. This wasn't supposed to happen." She turned away from him,

Matt circled her with one large step, blocking her path, "What wasn't supposed to happen?"

"This!" Lucy never thought this was even possible. Falling into a situation like this, a relationship that was the seed to something great but wouldn't ever break the surface of the dirt, damned to remain six feet underground forever.

"My schizophrenia medications affected my liver."

"You said you stopped taking them."

"The damage was already done."

A long silence.

A bulky figure carrying a woman through fog...

Matt didn't say anything, he also didn't take his eyes off Lucy, didn't blink once.

Shadows of tombstones in the mist...

He'd been speared through the chest. Blood pooling under his shirt. Maybe Lucy was the one who saw it, but she knew Matt could feel it. "You're unbelievable."

"I didn't know how to say it. Or when," Lucy huffed. He didn't deserve this, she "I just didn't have the balls to tell you."

Matt's expression hardened. "How long?"

"Less than a year," Lucy mumbled.

"No, how long did you know?"

Shit. Well, there was no stopping this bus before it crashed. Lucy just wished the impact would end the pain, though she had a feeling it was this mistake right here that was her biggest yet. It was never Lucifera who'd been ruining Lucy's life, it was Lucy. All Lucy, the master at the wheel navigating into every brick wall she could find since day one. And for what?

"It's why I came to Ireland. To get away from everything." She shook her head. "So much for *magic*."

That was a knife twisted in Matt's heart. And hell, it cut Lucy just the same.

Matt took a long time to choose his next words, and all he ended up saying was, "Goodbye Lucy," then he left.

Lucifera's steps came up behind Lucy, she smelled her perfume. Something that Lucy used to love but was discontinued ages ago. That was a first. "I tried to save you from this," said Lucifera.

Lucy turned and pushed Lucifera to the ground. She didn't expect it to work, but it did. She was done questioning. Sure, Lucy messed up a lot. But she was so frustrated and there was no hope of reprieve, just the end. If her mind was going to attack her, she'd attack back, she was livid. "That little stunt was uncalled for!"

Lucifera stared up at her. "It wasn't me!"

"It's all you. Tricking me, all the time," she smacked the sides of her head, grabbing fistfuls of hair.

"It *wasn't* me!"

"It's so much worse," said Lucy, "because Matt actually might have been something special. He didn't care about all this *shit!* And now it doesn't even make a difference!"

"Too good to be true, eh?" A flash of anger in Lucifera's eyes.

"What's that supposed to mean?"

"You know exactly what it's supposed to mean!"

Tears rolled down Lucy's cheeks, this was too much. She turned and padded down the other way. Lucifera had gotten in her head. Rushing down the stairs of the ruin, Lucy began sobbing uncontrollably as she sat on a stone out there. The tears were a tiny reprieve. There was nothing else she could do, just accept and move on. That was her life now. Accepting what was being thrown at her. The lack of control was impossible to swallow.

Her phone buzzed. She blinked a few tears away to see the screen, controlled her voice best she could. "Hi Mum."

She wanted to get away from Mary when this all started. Now all she wanted was a hug from her.

"I just landed in Dublin. What's the name of your hotel?"

"What? Mum, why?" Lucy wiped her face.

"You didn't take half my calls; you could have been dead for all I know!"

"I'm fine Mum. I just—"

"Where are you!?"

A pause from Lucy. "I'm in Waterford."

"She's in Waterford. Go!" Mary was likely ordering a taxi driver. "Lucy, listen to me. Don't do anything stupid, all right? You're a smart woman. Be logical. Please. I'm here for you. Whatever's going on, we're going to talk through it. Just don't go anywhere. Wait for me, love, I'll call you when I'm there." Mary sounded beyond worried, as if Lucy was a flight risk. Well, she supposed she was.

"I miss you," Mary said.

"I'll be here Mum, don't worry," Lucy reassured. "I missed you, too." She hung up. Over her shoulder, she looked back at the entrance to the castle, considering going back in.

Dunhill Chalet, the inn where Lucy was staying while out here visiting the castle, was a rustic hillside building that looked like it fell out of the middle ages. The wooden floors and beams made for a cosy interior.

Lying on her back, staring at the ceiling of her room, Lucy was exhausted. From the crumpled tissues, she could tell she'd been crying a lot, because she didn't really remember that well. It was a bit of a haze.

"Stupid pills..." she muttered. "Stupid Dr Gray. Stupid bloody Dearg Due!" Like the banshee she'd been told about, Lucy let out an unintelligible scream.

She uses her feet to feel for vibrations in the ground, hoping for a plump juicy one this time. Other crows peck at the grass, too. A couple turn their beady black eyes curiously towards the chalet. So does she. She hops in the direction, considering flying over to the window to have a look at who'd caused the high-pitched sound. Then she spears the grass with her sharp beak, catching a juicy worm.

- Chapter Eight -
"Pink, Yellow, Red"

The moon showed her face intermittently through clouds up above. Matt hadn't come back since their falling out at Dunhill Castle. Lucy didn't have the face to go talk to him. She'd simply called a taxi to get back to the chalet after Mary had called. Matt's car was still parked out there when she left. If he wanted to see her, he would have called.

She'd never lied to someone like that. It was a betrayal she herself most likely couldn't have forgiven. Lucy never gave him the choice. It started out as nothing serious, then became the toughest thing she had to do. When she was too far in, her voices hit hard.

A knock came at the door to her room. A small part of her wished it was him, though she knew better. Two and a half hours had passed since she spoke to her mother, who'd just arrived at Dublin Airport. Lucy opened the door for Mary. "Hi Mum."

Mary stared at her for a second, looked like she didn't believe her eyes. Lucy could relate. She wasn't sure what to believe anymore.

Mary slapped Lucy across the face. "Don't *ever* do that again."

Lucy was so exhausted she didn't react much more than glaring at Mary half-heartedly.

Not waiting for a response, Mary pulled her daughter close into an embrace. She began jerking with quiet sobs.

Once the overpowering, complicated feelings had dissipated, and the sun had set, they both sat on the bed. Mary's suitcase lay open at the foot, clothes in a small heap.

Pouring water from a bottle on the bedside table, Mary filled a disposable cup for Lucy, handed it to her with a couple of pills. One yellow clozapine. One pink citalopram. For a long while Lucy stared at them. What was this all for?

"Lucy…" Mary egged her on. Gently.

"I don't want to, Mum."

Mary was tentative, seeming somewhat suspicious. Lucy couldn't blame her. If she were in her shoes, she wouldn't know how to have dealt with everything. "I'm sorry I've been so selfish, Mum"

"Are they here now?"

This again. Lucy sighed irritated, "Can't you just leave it be, Mum. Let's have a somewhat normal conversation. Please? I've been managing fine."

"You don't know what's real and what isn't."

"I do. I can tell. Whenever something's off it's in the 'Otherworld' and I know the difference."

"Lucy…I spoke with Dr Gray."

"Mum, those pills are the reason I'm in this situation." Lucy felt her chest tightening from the inside.

"I need you to listen to me. Please." Mary spoke tentatively, like she was trying to approach a deer without spooking it.

"Why are you talking like that?"

"Because you're not making any sense, dear," Mary said. "You quit your job, ran away from home on a whim, for what? Because Dr Gray is retiring? There are plenty of other good doctors out there."

"What the *hell* are you on about?"

"Why did you come to Ireland?"

"Because I'm dying from the medication."

Mary nodded slowly, tearing up. "Lucy, I spoke to Dr Gray. He never told you anything of the sort."

"What's this?" her head began to swim. It was all a ruse? The lot of it? So every decision she made—all the carelessness and recklessness without thinking about what tomorrow would bring, because there was no tomorrow, was all just... Lucy.

"I called him after you gave me the news. Pleaded with him for a liver transplant. He had no idea why."

"No, no, no, I was there—I heard him—he told me I have agranulocytosis, cirrhosis of the liver..."

"Dr Gray said I should give you some space," Mary persisted, "which was obviously a *grand* mistake because you went off to bloody Ireland!"

"Mum!" Lucy shouted. This couldn't be real. It couldn't. And yet, it was. It had to be. Mary was right, for once. Lucy hadn't known what was real and what wasn't, because she was swimming in a haze of confusion, lying to herself. Pretending that burying a figurative part of her would make any difference. Looking back, she always knew. Whether she liked it or not, her conscience had a voice and a face that looked just like hers. "I scoured the internet and found nothing to help. I saw it with my own eyes!" Something still didn't make sense. What was different then and now? How could she tell that this was real? Well, for one, Mary was here—she'd never been part of a hallucination.

Mary nodded slowly at her, clearly sorrowful and petrified of witnessing her daughter in this state.

"I'm missing something."

"Lucy—"

"Shh. Hold on." Lucy slowly raised a hand; she needed to wrap her head around this. "I *saw* it with my own eyes. Lucifera never lied to me," it hit her like a double-decker bus. Sure, she tricked Lucy a whole lot. But *never* did she lie. Not once. From the very beginning, she swung an axe at Dr Gray's neck.

"Mum," Lucy said very, very slowly, still staring at the newcomer. "What does Dr Gray look like?"

"What!?" Who are you looking at?"

"Show me a picture of Dr Gray."

"You need to snap out of—"

"Just search it online!"

Grudgingly, Mary did. "There!"

Someone clapped, emerged from the bathroom behind Mary. At first, it was just a tall shadow with red eyes, creeping out the dark quarters. The new voice inspired by Dracula that tricked Lucy into telling Matt the truth. Lucy found that she was still angry at him, and

as he stepped into the light, Lucy recognised the face.

Dr Gray.

Dr Gray—or more precisely—Vlad the Impaler, grinned playfully at Lucy. That blood red tunic of his, lace up shirt, boots, the sword on his hip, all something from another time, another world.

Lucy checked the photo, looked back at the man she thought was Dr Gray until now. They weren't even slightly similar.

The *real* Dr Gray had short ginger hair, a goatee, horn-rimmed glasses—not even close to this grey-haired man she was convinced she'd been treated by. Vlad raised his eyebrows, shrugged.

"Holy shit!" Lu rang out.

"I did not see this coming..." Luce gasped.

Lucy glared at Lucifera, who'd showed herself along with Lucinda. "Was this your idea?"

"No," Lucifera snarled.

Lucinda shook her head, too.

"Lucy stop talking to them!" Mary screeched.

"You did all this." Lucy turned on Vlad. "Made me believe I was dying?"

"You needed to accept who you are, Lucinda," he said simply.

"Why the hell would you care?"

Mary looked like she might shake out of her skin. "Lucy, don't talk to them, you'll get back into a rut—"

"Hold on, Mum," Lucy said firmly.

"You're a special lass," Vlad said. "Different. Believing you were sick, your most special part villainised. I relate to being villainised."

Mary stepped right in front of Lucy's face. "That is *enough!*" she shrieked again, shaking little angry fists in the air.

"Mum, stop it!" Lucy begged. "I know this freaks you out, but it's important! Just trust me for once, all right!?" She pushed past her.

"No! I will not stop! You are my daughter, and I am here to help save you from this madness!"

"It's not madness! Well—it's—" Lucy took a few deep breaths. Then it sank in. "I'm not dying... I'm not dying..."

The others all smiled around her, even Lu and Luce's reflections were visible in the blank TV screen. Lucy burst into tears of joy. She hugged her mother tight. The woman was hardly holding herself together. She seemed wrung out to the last drop.

She held Lucy's face in her hands. "My beautiful Lucinda."

Vlad was gone. The wall cracked behind Mary just a sliver, maybe it spread beyond that, though Lucy chose not to look.

It was quiet in Lucy's head. Too quiet. She'd gotten used to the noise and a nagging suspicion fluttered in the pit of her belly. Knowing her own brain—this was too easy. To ignore it and put up pretenses for Mary, she'd turned on the TV, leaving a music channel on in the background, low and soothing. Lucy crossed the room to a tiny refrigerator.

"I've made a batch of sack mead. Give it a taste."

Bringing a thermos back to bed where her mother sat with her feet up, Lucy poured a swig in a disposable cup.

Mary cocked her head, amused. For a split-second, her eyes flicked to the pills that Lucy left on the bedside table.

"Smells good," was all Mary said.

There was no way she didn't care about the rules anymore, but it seemed to Lucy that more than that, right now she just wanted to be with her daughter. Lucy appreciated it, because she felt just a little closer to her mother since the rift had cracked open between them and grown wider over the years, just like those snaking fissures in Lucy's visions.

Joining Mary on the bed, Lucy filled her own cup. She watched her mother for a reaction as she sipped the mead.

"That is bloody good." Mary smacked her lips. "How old is it?"

"A week."

She was clearly impressed. "Lucy, you know what?" The woman smiled suddenly. She seemed to have an idea, getting fully into it. "Maybe your quitting your job is a blessing in disguise. This tastes fantastic and it's not even aged. You've got a knack for this stuff."

As her mother took another sip of unaged mead, Lucy leaned back on the headrest, stared at the pink and yellow pills. She plucked them up decisively. Lucifera reappeared, shaking her head indignantly.

"Don't," she begged.

Lucy washed the meds down with a sip of water, leaving her cup of mead untouched.

Lucy and Mary shared the only bed in the room that night. It had been a long time since Lucy slept this well.

Even since before she got the bad news, she hadn't rested so peacefully.

Until something clattered outside.

She kept her eyes closed, hoping to fall into that blissful slumber again.

A stone hit the window.

Annoyed, and just a little curious, Lucy got up to check it out. Squinting through the curtain, she saw a familiar silhouette.

"How did you find me?"

She'd switched to another room, asked the clerk at the front not to tell anyone where she was. Quietly, she tiptoed out into the hall. Mary shifted in her sleep but didn't wake. Lucy closed the door after her with a soft *click*.

Outside the chalet, grass rose and dipped into dark mountains that disappeared in the fog. Back towards her, Matt was looking into the mist.

"Matt, I'm sorry I just left like that—"

A cold, scratchy voice responded. "I'm afraid it's not Matt, my dear."

"Oh, come on..." Lucy groaned. "I took the medicine."

"Medicine stops you from seeing what's *not* real," Vlad taunted.

"What's with you man? Where did you even come from," Lucy snapped.

He flicked Lucy's forehead, chuckled. "I've always been here, you've just never paid attention, Lucy. Your Matt's in trouble."

Shaking her head, Lucy turned away from Vlad.

Lucifera faced her, anxious. "Listen to him."

"Like I'm going to trust you?"

Lucifera tried to contain her frustration, mostly failing. "He's not making this up."

"I see, you're both working together. First trick me into telling Matt—"

"I have *never* lied to you," Lucifera insisted. "I've messed with you—profusely—but I never lied."

Lucy almost bought it.

Lucinda showed up. "What's your gut tell you, Lucy?"

Lucy took a beat to work through this.

"She never lied to her?" Luce asked.

"Never," Lu replied.

"Not even once?"

"Not once."

"I just got my life back," Lucy said resolutely "If this is some game of yours…" she turned to Lucifera.

Lucifera shook her head adamantly, "It's not, I swear."

"I'm sorry my dear," Vlad said, "but you'll have to do this alone. I can't face her; I never really could."

"What?" Lucy frowned.

And he was gone.

"And I'm supposed to be the weirdo." Lucy sighed heavily.

At the reception desk, she approached the Dunhill clerk whom she'd booked the room from earlier. Just behind her, the other two Lucies kept close.

"Excuse me."

"Hello miss!" This one was a happy lad. Still wide awake and eager to serve at 3 a.m. He set down his phone, paused whatever he was watching and removed his earphones, giving Lucy his full attention.

"Did anyone come looking for me?" she asked.

"Er... the man... yes! He asked about a British blonde woman."

"Oh good! Where is he?"

"He left."

"When?"

"About..." The clerk checked his watch. "...half an hour ago. Don't worry though, I don't think he'll come back to bother you. He looked a little, you know." The clerk mimicked knocking down a drink.

"Shit!" Lucy grimaced. "Did he say where he was going?"

He shrugged. "No. Though he did seem to think you were a princess of sorts."

"Come again?"

"Thought he might find you in a castle."

"Thank you!"

Lucy got on her cell immediately.

Unstrapped, Lucy sat in the front seat, leaning forward, peering intently out the windscreen. Lucinda and Lucifera in the back. The puffy-eyed taxi driver looked at Lucy like she was crazy. He also looked like he was far too tired to be driving, blinking repeatedly, rubbing his face. Yawning.

Spotting Matt's car parked on the side of the road, Lucy jumped up with excitement, "There!"

The driver slammed the brakes. Lucy hit her head on the windscreen, not too hard, though.

"Ow! Damnit." She rushed out. Everyone but the driver followed her. He called after Lucy.

"Hey! Hey!"

All three of her turned.

"Money!"

"Just wait here a couple of minutes, all right?" she asked.

He sighed in frustration, "Yeah, yeah, all right..."

Lucy took a step in the direction of the forest. "Wait!"

The driver zoomed off, cursing rampantly.

"Son of a bitch!"

Lucy led the way, rushing through the crowded trail, a nettle of trees and bushes. She held her elbows close.

"Just don't let there be spiders," Lu's voice echoed in a wishful tremor.

Lucy turned on her phone's flashlight. For now, everything was dark. Lucy had no idea where to go. It all looked the same. As they trekked deeper, she started doubting what she was doing. Lucinda walked up beside her. "What are you thinking, lass?"

"I'm scared of what I'll find."

Lucifera came close. "He'll be all right. I can feel it."

Lucy still couldn't bring herself to trust her fully. "You know, I kind of missed you."

"Wow, only took a little bit of death and a smidge of Dracula to get you there.," Lucifera said.

"Well, I can be stubborn," Lucy retorted. "Like someone else I know." They hadn't bantered like this in forever, if it had always been like this, Lucy would never had taken the pills in the first place. She also probably would have never met Matt.

"Hey Luce?"

"Hmm?" Lucifera replied, knowing that the shorthand was meant for her this time.

"You think everything happens for a reason?"

"*Shhh! Shhh!*" the voices urged.

All eyes went to the front.

"What the hell?" Lucy whispered.

Voices. Female voices, but not Lucy's. A song.

Moving slowly, tentatively, the small group padded on, brushing aside some low hanging leaves. An orange light flickered up ahead.

"Here," Lucinda handed Lucy a glass bottle. Blackness swirled inside. It was the same one with the trapped *bánánach* from her first night in Ireland.

"Where'd you get this?" Lucy was stunned. "How?"

"The crow that died on the road yesterday," Lucinda said. "A rift opened when your blood mixed, it called her through, bridging between your world and the Otherworld. You're a little in both now." She pushed the bottle at her. "You may yet need it."

Lucy was trying to remember when she'd taken the bottle. Or was this just another hallucination? She didn't know what the hell Lucinda was ranting on about. She always mentioned odd folkloric things that didn't make sense. Then again, this was all so strange, she'd go with just about anything at this point.

Dunhill Castle looked ominous in the dark. Especially when there was a woman in red standing there, singing in no particular language. Vocalising. Four torches stuck out the ground, flames illuminating the scene. The woman chanted on, her back to Lucy.

Something snorted a short distance to Lucy's right. Her silent friend, the Gravedigger. Holding his shovel as if it were a trident. Lucy squinted, following his line of sight.

"Matt..."

He lay on a large flat stone, like an altar. Eyes closed, Matt's chest pumped up and down.

The horned Gravedigger shifted his horizontal ram-pupils in Lucy's direction. Locked eyes with her. Didn't move. Snorted slightly.

Damn he was creepy. Where the hell did her brain conjure this thing from? But she never felt threatened by him. He was always just there. Doing his own thing in the Otherworld. Probably the most placid of Lucy's visions.

The woman in red didn't notice a thing. Her lovely song began to sound eerie, echoing with unnatural reverb.

"This is the weirdest it's ever been," Lucy whispered to Lucinda and Lucifera. "What do we do? What is this?"

"Dearg Due," Lucinda said slowly.

"Irish Vampire Bitch," Lucifera added.

Lucy looked at the woman in red again.

"She's the one Vlad was talking about. His woman." The same story that Lucinda was telling Lucy about while she initially started working on cleaning up the meadery.

Cold, scratchy laughing from up ahead. "Welcome, Lucy," said the Dearg Due.

Lucy led, with the other two close behind. The Gravedigger hung back, a mythical sentry, not interfering.

"Do we have to do this?" Lucy said.

"Do you know my story?" Dearg Due turned to face her, guarding Matt's unconscious body.

"Lucinda mentioned something."

"Bram Stoker sought inspiration from me."

"Vlad says otherwise," Lucy murmured.

"Vlad's a coward!" Dearg Due spat. "Can't even face me after so many years. He's the one who saved me, but I guess I was too much for him."

"What are you doing?" Lucy asked impatiently.

"I'm getting out, Lucy," her words were venom. "Not another day spent in this prison of the Otherworld. I will have my blood. Whether it's you or him," she pointed at Matt, "A life for a life, and I will be free."

Lucy exchanged a look with the other two.

"Just like my father did, when he sold me to that chieftain. But I killed him. Killed them all. Taught them their lesson. Same one I'll teach you here tonight." The Dearg Due bent down to Matt's neck.

"Strange..." Lucy said. She always considered the Otherworld a paradise of sorts, until she started taking her meds and shutting out the others, when it became her bane.

"Lucy!" Lucifera urged, "She'll kill him—the *bánánach*!"

"Here goes my last shred of sanity," Lucy tossed the water bottle at the base of the flat rock. Glass shattered. The swirling shadows of the *bánánach* escaped with a wail, distracting the Dearg Due.

Lucy gawked at the two mythical creatures tussle with each other. It was quite a sight, she couldn't believe how vivid and utterly wild this whole vision was, better than any CGI she'd ever seen. "This is insane."

"Come on, Lass!" Lucinda tugged on her.

"Hurry up!" Lucifera followed.

The three of them rushed to Matt's side. Lucy tried to wake him. The Dearg Due disentangled from the *bánánach,* knocking Lucy down. That shouldn't happen. Her cognitive mind told her that she must have tripped. The woman in red plonked herself on Lucy's back and grabbed her neck from behind in a chokehold, strangling her. Lucy struggled for air. She felt her eyes bulge, the veins in her forehead about to burst as she gasped. Was there someone else here with her? It shouldn't be this bad—she took her meds. Unless...

Frantic, like a cat on its back, Lucy clawed behind her, managing to poke the Dearg Due in her eye. The creature screamed. Furious, she closed harder around Lucy's windpipe. Lucinda and Lucifera fended off the wild *bánánach* soaring at them, screeching, snapping her inhumanly wide jaws like a starved piranha.

With a hollow metallic *clang*, the Dearg Due went flying off Lucy. The Gravedigger readjusted his shovel and batted at her. The *bánánach* flew at him mindlessly.

Catching her breath, Lucy grabbed Matt at the armpit. "I've completely lost it!"

He had a bloodstain on the side of his head where he'd been knocked. She started hauling him off the rock. Lucinda took the other shoulder, and Lucifera the legs. Together they carried him out of there, tracing their steps back where they came. It was a hell of a haul, and Lucy knew that she was physically doing all the work herself. The adrenaline helped her drag him all the way. They were almost at the lot, Matt's car just a few steps away.

Vengeful, with a wild, evil look, the Dearg Due charged at them, knocking Lucy off her feet. The others tried to help. Lucifera barreled at the Dearg Due, who pounced on Lucy. She smacked a stone to her head, tackled her to the ground. It didn't do much, but it did push her off balance for a brief snippet.

"Get Matt," Lucifera shouted, "and get out!"

She didn't have to ask twice. Lucy and Lucinda dragged the intoxicated Matt to the car. As soon as this was all over Lucy could go back to normal. Mostly. But would it ever really end?

"She's going to follow us!" Lucy huffed.

"We'll have to reseal the rift," Lucinda said.

"How?"

She and Lucinda shoved Matt in the back seat. Lucifera bolted.

Lucy got behind the wheel. "Keys—in his pockets!"

Lucinda rummaged around. "Here!"

The engine rumbled to life. "Get in!" Lucy yelled. Lucinda hopped in the passenger seat. Lucifera was right behind—but the Dearg Due grabbed her back by the neck.

Instinctively, Lucy jumped out the car. Lucifera yelled, clawing at the vice grip on her throat. "Lucy!" she called out.

Crunch.

Lucy wailed, like a banshee, tripping onto the road. This couldn't happen. She was watching Lucifera—herself—dead. Head hanging limp. Eyes wide, blank.

"Lucy!" she croaked. On her knees, she was already crawling towards her.

She wept like a child, unable to breathe. The shock was too much, all too sudden. This shouldn't happen. The Dearg Due shouldn't be standing there smirking wickedly, taking slow deliberate steps toward her. Lucinda pulled her to her feet.

"Get your arse in that car!"

"We have to get Lucifera!" Lucy wouldn't move. "I'm not going anywhere without her."

Lucinda tugged persistently, but her grip was weakening with every pull. "You want us to be next?"

Broken, confused, Lucy found herself back in the vehicle. She didn't remember when she started driving.. In the rearview mirror, Lucifera lay motionless on the tarmac. Lucy saw her own reflection shrinking away, dead on the ground, as the Gravedigger, one horn missing now, pounced on the Dearg Due with his shovel at full force.

Lucinda didn't say a word. Matt breathed deeply, starting to come to.

Lucinda wiped her eyes. Lucy sobbed quietly, eyes redder than ever, her vision so blurry that it wasn't the smartest idea to carry on driving, yet she wasn't thinking clearly.

"The rift is closed." Lucinda sounded detached. "I can feel it."

"She was my best friend," Lucy choked.

"She loved you."

Lucy didn't speak. The car swerved a little. "She—can't—be gone—" even after Lucy had buried her voices, she always knew they were there, in the background. Now something was missing. She'd lost a friend.

"The rift is closed," Lucinda said blankly. "She closed it."

Every nuance in the uneven road made Lucy feel like she was in a rattling cage that was falling apart piece by piece.

Matt woke, shaking his head, holding it in pain. "Lucy?" he asked, still groggy. When he took his hand away from his head, it was bloody.

- Chapter Nine -
"Crow's Song"

Coming out the hospital, Matt joined Lucy in the car. She wore sunglasses even though it was an overcast morning. Her head hurt like hell, the white light filtering through the clouds was like a giant surgeon's fluorescent glaring at her.

They drove in silence for a while, until Lucy reached an intersection.

"Lucy..." Matt said, tentative.

Outside on a road sign was a crow pecking under its wing, hopping a little, looking about, going back to cleaning. She watched the black bird longingly.

"I'm sorry," Matt said.

"It's not your fault." Her eyes were still on the bird. "Why did you go back into the woods?"

"I thought I saw you there. In that red cardigan of yours."

Lucy tore away from the crow. What did he just say?

"I was a little buzzed and I followed." Matt shook his head, ashamed. "I slipped, I guess... How did you know I was out there?"

"The clerk at the chalet said you went looking for me at the castle."

"Aye..."

"Matt, I have some good news to share with you." When she first found out, she imagined how she might break it to him. Now she just said it flatly. "I'm not sick."

"What do you mean?"

"I'm not dying."

Matt was pensive for long, She thought he might be suspicious. "This is big. You found a cure?" His posture changed, full of hope , all in.

Despite it all he was still here. Somehow. She motioned with her hand beside her head."It was part of my..."

"Magic?" Matt finished for her. He looked so relieved. Lucy shrugged. Sure, that was a good an explanation as any.

Matt pulled her close, hugged her for a long time, like he missed her. They held on as if they were never going to see each other again.

The crow's wings ruffle as it takes flight off the road sign, gliding through the landscape, the scenery moves past like paint spilling on a canvas, indiscernible... Clouds... Mist...

Crows squawking. Tombstones. Fog. Soft snarling breaths...

Sunlight moved through fog like water at Brompton Cemetery. Tranquil. In front of that moss-covered tombstone that read *Lu, Luce, Lucy, Lucinda*, Lucy and Mary paid their respects.

"Thank you for coming, Mum."

"Talking to me like I'm some stranger!?" Mary gasped. "I'm your mother, Lucy. Of course I'm here."

"I know it's hard for you, letting me do this."

"Listen, if you're happy, I'm happy. I've come to realise that normal ain't that interesting anyway, is it?" Rather than the anger it stemmed from in the past, Mary seemed mischievous when she asked it this time. "Are they here now?"

Lucy nodded. Lucinda stood beside her, quietly. Wearing black.

Mary said, "I'll give you a moment, then." She left, walking past Matt, who appeared through the fog. He nodded a greeting at her as she passed.

He came and stood solemnly by Lucy.

"I got my life back," she said. "Just like that. Kind of like starting over." Lucy glanced at Lucinda. Grinned half-heartedly.

"Is she ever going to come back?" Matt asked.

"No. No, she isn't."

"What is it?" Matt said. "What are you thinking?"

"Just something Lucifera said," Lucy got a light whiff of his cologne in the breeze.

"Something she said about me?" he asked.

Lucy nodded, remembering that evening on the bench vividly.

"You look like you're trying to decide something. What's the verdict?"

"I'm trusting myself," she said. It was a decision, no more doubt.

A crow landed on the tombstone.

"No way," Luce echoed. *"You think—"*

"Luce..." Lu said gently.

"Just hoping," Luce sighed.

"I know, me too," Lucy whispered. Matt didn't ask questions. She glanced at him to gauge his reaction. Did he see it, too?

"Crows were her favourite birds."

"Maybe she's here now," Matt suggested. "Maybe that's her."

Lucy smiled. Maybe it was true, maybe it wasn't. It didn't matter. What she was doing might seem ridiculous. But felt right. "I—" She choked up, looking at the crow. "I love you."

It stared back unwavering. Poker-faced.

Matt came a little closer to her. "I want you to tell me all about her. When you're ready."

Lucy drew a deep breath, her face close to Matt's, taking in his scent.

"She loved the name Lucifera. Even though she pretended she didn't. She liked anything mischievous like that." When Lucy neared the tombstone, the crow perched atop it didn't get spooked. She pulled a paint marker out her pocket.

Scratching on the tombstone in red, Lucy changed the engraved *Lucy* to *Lucifera*. As she did, the elegant, silver bracelet with a crow charm slipped out from under her sleeve. Stepping back, Lucy nodded in approval. Lucinda grinned wistfully.

Matt watched in silence. He didn't hear the footsteps that followed this. Didn't see the one-horned Gravedigger arrive from behind a tree. Breath misting through his flared nostrils as he padded through the mist, carrying a woman in white.

Lucifera.

Lucy's heart leapt.

Lucinda gasped, started, took a step forward.

It looked like Lucifera might be asleep, in a white dress. Beautiful as ever. Lucy was rooted to the spot in awe. The Gravedigger bent on one knee and placed her on the earth. Lucifera sank in as if it were water, peacefully.

Tears filled Lucy's eyes. She, too, knelt down and touched the dewed earth. Lucinda did the same. They shared a smile. A mix of sorrow and closure. Lucifera wasn't just tossed somewhere on a street in Ireland. She was here now. Matt noticed Lucy staring at one spot. He had the sense to say nothing, and let her have this moment.

The Gravedigger nodded once to Lucy, then walked away.

The crow squawked, flew off. A 'thank you,' she imagined. She straightened, inhaling deeply. At last, there was peace in her life. Real peace.

Lucinda walked behind her. Then, it was just Lucy and Matt. He put his arm around her shoulder, they went down the path, Lucy snuggling close to her beloved.

Thunder echoes as they pace along, rain begins trickling, the lovers pass through an arched wooden door far up ahead. Rain patters the door, bringing out darker hues of wood. For a long while, it's just thunder and rain. Then footsteps splosh, someone opens the door with a ding, getting inside. Only their lower half is visible as they brush past Léon the

Chinese evergreen. There's a little greeting sign on his pot, the door closes.

A few short beats, and another set of footsteps. Light spills out from inside. Chatter, music, Léon's sign becomes visible again as the patron brushes past: 'Welcome to Crow's Song Meadery! Grand Opening!' Door closes. Rain and thunder.

Another patron in a white dress enters.

Thunder.

Lightning.

Someone hums as they near the door. A man's voice, "Everything for love..." He's wearing lace-up boots, a red tunic. Pushes through the door with a ding. Léon greets faithfully. A snippet of laughter from inside.

The door's shut again, leaving out the storm.

Finally, heavy footsteps thump closer to the entrance. A pair of legs stands there unmoving in front of the meadery. A familiar huff, a snort.

ABOUT THE AUTHOR

Originally from South Africa, Adir E Golan moved to the US where he earned his BA in English and Creative Writing and an MFA in Screenwriting. If he's not at a keyboard, he's probably brewing a fresh carboy of mead or trying his hand at a batch of homemade chocolate. He is currently working on his next book.

X: @adiregolan
TikTok/YouTube: @manmaedfables

www.ingramcontent.com/pod-product-compliance
Lightning Source LLC
Chambersburg PA
CBHW030539130626
46552CB00006B/2328